Murder and Meringue Cake

A BITE-SIZED BAKERY COZY MYSTERY BOOK 4

ROSIE A. POINT

Murder and Meringue Cake

A Bite-sized Bakery Cozy Mystery Book 4

You're invited!

Hi there, reader!

I'd like to formally invite you to join my awesome community of readers. We love to chat about cozy mysteries, cooking, and pets.

It's super fun because I get to share chapters from yet-to-be-released books, fun recipes, pictures, and do giveaways with the people who enjoy my stories the most.

So whether you're a new reader or you've been enjoying my stories for a while, you can catch up with other like-minded readers, and get lots of cool content by visiting my website at *www.rosiepointbooks.com* and signing up for my mailing list.

Or simply search for me on *www.bookbub.com* and follow me there.

I look forward to getting to know you better.

Let's get into the story!

Yours,
Rosie

One

"HAPPY BIRTHDAY TO YOU! HAPPY BIRTHDAY TO you," Bee sang, swaying from side-to-side in the food truck. The sun had just started setting, casting its oranges and pinks over the Maine sky and the ocean waves. The beach was placid, the benches in front of our truck empty, and the customers lining up to get their last fix of sweet treats.

We were due to close up shop any second, and I anticipated a night of quiet contemplation, Sam's delicious dinner at the guesthouse, and a bubble bath.

But Bee had other plans.

"Happy birthday to you," my friend continued. "Come on. Everybody sing along."

My cheeks grew warm as the last customers of the day

1

—all lined up in front of the Bite-sized Bakery food truck —cheered and clapped and sang along.

"Bee," I said, "thank you, but this is not necessary."

"Of course it's necessary," she replied. "It's not every day that a woman turns thirty-seven!" Bee grinned and brought out a cupcake on a plate. She had placed a magenta candle in its center and a cherry off to one side on top of creamy white frosting. "I hope you don't mind, folks, but it's time we celebrate Ruby's birthday."

The customers applauded again.

"You don't have to do this." I couldn't help smiling though. I had never liked my birthday. I'd never had a particularly memorable one, and I didn't see any reason to go ahead and celebrate a day when I was another year older.

Not that there was anything wrong with getting old. At least I'd started living my dream.

But this type of thing *was* important to Bee. The customers huddled closer to the truck's window, watching as my friend lit the candle for me to blow out. I took a breath and blew out the merry flame to cheers and shouts.

"Thank you all, so much," I said, smiling. "And thank you, Bee."

"It's just a cupcake, Rubes. I've got a gift for you waiting back at the Oceanside."

"You really shouldn't have."

Bee had made up her mind. She wanted to spoil me for my birthday. And I wouldn't deny her that if it meant so much to her.

We finished up serving the last of the folks waiting for their treats and coffees or hot chocolates. Each of them wished me a happy birthday then hurried off into the evening, the sky purpling like the lavender dusting on a donut.

The wind was still, but it was cold enough that I needed a thick coat to keep me warm outside the truck.

"Are you ready to go?" Bee rubbed her hands together and grinned.

"Yes, I am," I replied. "Why?" I tilted my head to one side. "You're acting strangely."

"I'm not. I'm just excited to celebrate your birthday with you," Bee said, the tip of her nose red. She'd only just recovered from the flu the week before and had a few sniffs to get over still. "And to give you your gift."

"Bee, you know you don't need to go wasting your money on me." I paid her well—she was a fantastic baker —and we had loads of fun working together. I considered her a good friend, but that didn't mean I wanted her spending her money on me.

"You don't like birthdays, do you?" Bee asked, as we shut the side window on the food truck and made our way around to the front of it. We got inside, and I sighed, shutting my door and then clipping my seatbelt into place.

"What gives you that idea?" I asked.

"Oh, maybe it's the fact that you look more sad than happy. And you went pink as a peach when we sang happy birthday to you."

I shrugged. "I'm not used to all that attention. And I've never really celebrated my birthday before."

"You haven't?" Bee was incredulous. "Not even when you were little?"

"Sometimes I'd have cake, but it was never a big deal. My parents had other things to worry about, like finances. Or deciding whether they wanted to stay together or not."

"Eek. Sorry, I didn't know."

"Of course you didn't," I said. "We don't talk about boring stuff like this."

"It's not boring, Ruby." Bee clipped on her seatbelt. "But if you don't want to do anything for your birthday, that's fine. We don't have to." She shifted and brought her phone out of her pocket.

"No. Let's do what you wanted to do. That sounds fun. Different." The last time I'd celebrated a birthday, it had been with my ex-fiancé, Daniel, and that hadn't exactly gone according to plan either. In that he'd never turned up for the celebration.

Instead, he'd disappeared. And the only way I'd discovered he was still OK and alive was through his family. But he didn't want to see me again.

I pressed my thumb to my ring finger and clicked my tongue. It was past time I forgot about him and all that silliness. "Come on," I said, "let's find out what Sam's cooked us for dinner. And then you can give me a birthday gift."

Bee slipped her phone back into her pocket and clapped her hands. "Perfect. I'm pretty nervous, though."

"You, nervous?"

"I know. So unlike me." She gave me her signature gap-toothed smile, tucking a few strands of silver hair behind her ears. "It must be the flu. It weakened not just my immune system but my emotional state. I wonder if they make medicine for that."

I laughed and steered the food truck down the road toward the Oceanside. I parked out front and frowned, peering up at the guesthouse. The lights were off. "That's strange. I thought Sam would be home."

"Maybe she forgot it was your birthday," Bee said. "She might have gone out to the Lobster Shack now that it's reopened."

"Heavens, I wonder if they're finally serving lobster there again."

"From what I heard, Benjamin's finally squashed his beef with the owner of the wharf. And that means lobster rolls," Bee said, licking her lips. "Let's go inside and see if she's there. If not, we can always go catch up with her at the Lobster Shack."

"That sounds good."

We got out of the truck, and Bee charged ahead of me, up the steps of the guesthouse. My frown deepened. It was so terribly quiet, and it sort of gave me the creeps. Halloween had been more than a week ago. The decorations had been taken down, and there hadn't been any other murders or incidents in Carmel Springs since then.

Bee unlocked the front door, and we entered.

"Goodness, it's dark," I said, stumbling in after her. "Usually Sam leaves the hall lights on."

"Here," Bee said and grabbed hold of my arm. She guided me a few steps into the guesthouse. "Almost. Just a few more steps."

"Huh? What are you talking about?"

The lights flicked on. At least twenty smiling faces greeted me followed by a roar of, "Surprise!"

I let out a cry, my hands flying to my face. Shock was quickly replaced by pleasure and excitement. My heart pounded away, and a giggle escaped me.

"Happy birthday," my friends chorused. Bee clapped and hopped up and down on the spot next to me.

"A surprise par—" But I cut off, my gaze shifting to the

long table where the gifts had been gathered. The gifts and something else. *Someone* else.

Another scream broke through the shouts and applause. And then another and another as the people in the room saw exactly what I had seen.

Detective Jones's body, draped across the sparkling wrapped gifts, the end of a silver knife sticking out of his back.

Two

I SAT DOWN HEAVILY IN ONE OF THE ARMCHAIRS —they had been pushed to the sides of the room to provide space for the party. Instead, they'd provided space for a dead body. Of a police officer.

I held a hand over my eyes to keep from looking at Jones's corpse. The screaming had stopped a while ago, but I didn't dare look. I was squeamish at the best of times, but this was beyond the pale. A police officer, stabbed and left on top of my birthday presents?

This is why I don't like birthday surprises. It was such a ridiculous thought I nearly laughed.

A whooping siren from outside brought me back to reality with a rather unpleasant bump. I dropped my hand and took in the room instead of the body.

People had backed up or filed toward the exit, though

no one seemed to have left yet. They couldn't, since Bee had taken it upon herself to block the doorway. "Nobody leaves," she said, "until the cops get here and interview everyone. The murderer might still be in this room."

Shocked cries rang out again. "You can't seriously believe that," said Kayla, one of the other guests at the Oceanside, pressing gloved fingers to her lips. The Carlingtons had already slipped on their coats.

"You never know," Bee replied, tapping the end of her nose. "It's always better to be safe. Now, I'm going to need you all to back away from the body and touch nothing in the living room. It's imperative we keep the scene as clean as possible. Stand out here in the hall. Ruby, that includes you."

"Good heavens." Millie, the editor of the local paper and our good friend, stopped next to me on her way out of the living room. "She's bossy, isn't she?"

"That's Bee." I got up and joined the line of folks filing into the entryway and the bottom floor hall that wound back toward the rooms, some of them still unoccupied. I would up standing next to Sam, the owner of the place.

Sam twirled strands of dark hair around her fingers then chewed on the ends. It was a nervous tick I'd never seen before, but, of course, she was freaked. A man had just been found dead in her guesthouse. This would be terrible for business.

Poor Sam. She'd been through a lot over the past few months. Not long ago, one of her guests had actually been murdered, though not in the guesthouse itself.

"It's going to be OK, Sam," I whispered, patting her on the back.

A short, sharp meow sounded between my ankles, and Trouble, the resident calico kitten, lifted himself onto his hind legs and rubbed his little face against my calf. He soon tottered to Sam, who swept him into her arms and kissed the top of his furry head.

"See, the cops are here," I said, and my mouth went a little dry.

The cops. Detective Jones had been a cop. And he'd also been the one and only "enemy" I had in town. He'd spent a lot of time investigating me, arresting me, and trying to pin murders on me instead of finding out who'd truly committed the crimes he'd been assigned.

And now he's dead in the guesthouse. At your surprise party. On your birthday.

This didn't look good. In fact, it looked kinda like ... did I dare even think it?

Detective Martin, who had been Jones's partner, entered and thanked Bee for ensuring folks didn't mess up the crime scene. People were split off into groups to have their statements taken, and Bee finally came over and joined me.

"I'm so sorry, Rubes," she whispered. "This was definitely *not* how I pictured your birthday party playing out."

"You and me both." Shoot, all I'd wanted was a bubble bath and a lobster roll. A cupcake too. "Who do you think could have done this?"

Bee shook her head, as Detective Martin emerged from the living room, handsome, pale, and clearly not happy about losing his partner. "Your guess is as good as mine. I mean, think about it. It's not like anyone in Carmel Springs liked the guy."

"Bee," I hissed.

"We certainly didn't. Millie didn't. Sam didn't. Shoot, even Shawn didn't." Shawn was the new chef and assistant at the Oceanside.

Bee was right, even though it made my skin crawl thinking that there was a murderer on the loose again. Someone who had the audacity to kill a homicide detective. Though, interestingly, he hadn't been in uniform at the time.

"Did you invite him to my surprise party?"

"What? Who?" Bee asked.

"Detective Jones. Was he supposed to be a guest?"

"No, of course not," Bee replied. "I don't know what he's doing here. For Pete's sake, I wouldn't have invited that man if you'd *asked* me to do it."

I nodded. "Then what was he doing here? At the

guesthouse. And in plain clothes? That doesn't make any sense."

Bee brought her cellphone out, drawing me away from the stragglers in the hall and the cops who had split up with people to take their statements. "I took photos of the scene just after it happened. Let me show you something."

"I really don't want to relive that 'surprise' moment, Bee."

"No, no, not that." Bee tapped on her screen and opened an image devoid of the dead body. "See? This was taken half an hour before we got back to the guesthouse. Sam sent it to me to let me know that they were ready for the big surprise."

"He's not there," I said, scanning the people, my new Carmel Springs friends, standing around the long table covered in gifts. "With the partygoers, I mean. Detective Jones isn't there."

"Exactly. And he's not on the table either." Bee shut off the screen as Detective Martin approached, lowering her voice to a hurried whisper. "That means that either someone killed him during the waiting period or put him in there when the lights had been shut off in preparation for your arrival."

The thought turned my stomach. One of the guests, or even someone else who might have access to the guesthouse tonight, had dragged the body in and put it on the table.

"Hello, Miss Holmes, Miss Pine." Detective Martin halted in front of us, his notepad out. "Mind if I ask you ladies a few questions?"

"Go ahead," Bee replied.

"We're sorry for your loss," I put in.

Detective Martin nodded by way of thanks but gave nothing more away. He kept his expression impassive as he walked us through questions about where we'd been, whether we had an alibi, and what exactly we'd seen.

"I last saw Detective Jones this morning," I said, while Martin took notes. "He came by the food truck to get a cookie."

"He did?" Bee asked. "Where was I?"

"You ran out to use the ladies' room on the pier," I replied. "Now that I think of it, he was acting a little different."

"How so?" Bee and Martin asked at the same time. The handsome detective gave her a deadpan stare. Bee clicked her tongue. "I'm just curious," she said.

"He's usually mean. And this morning he wasn't. I was too busy to think much about it at the time. He simply bought his cookie and stood near the benches, staring at the truck and eating his treat."

The detective scribbled the information down. "Is

there anything else you can think of? Anything strange or out of place regarding Jones or even the guesthouse?"

I chewed on the inside of my cheek, casting my thoughts back. "No, nothing."

"Nada," Bee agreed.

Martin withdrew a card from his pocket and handed it over. "Let me know if you think of anything else. Or if anything strange happens around here." And then he was gone, and I was left with his card, the scent of woodsy cologne on the air, and a hunger to figure out exactly who might have done this.

Jones's death made me a suspect. Bee too. And if Sam's guesthouse got in trouble … well, we certainly wouldn't let that happen.

Three

I YAWNED AND BLOCKED IT WITH THE BACK OF MY hand. I'd already had five cups of strong coffee this morning, but they hadn't helped one bit. Twice this morning, I'd given out wrong orders or incorrect change. Not exactly good for business.

But people didn't seem to mind much. They were more interested in talking about what had happened to Detective Jones. Gossip was rife, with interesting theories floating around as to who might have committed the crime.

I struggled to focus on them, though, since we'd hardly gotten a wink of sleep last night. And that was because the police had closed down the guesthouse for the night in order to investigate the crime scene and ascertain what had happened and how.

We'd been relocated to a motel just outside of town, and while it wasn't exactly uncomfortable, it had been difficult to fall asleep. Particularly, since Bee hadn't had her nightly coffee—she insisted it was the only way she could go to bed—and had kept me up with photos and theories of her own.

Jones dead.

It was crazy.

"Good morning," a woman said.

I blinked and looked up, holding my white paper coffee cup, the liquid now cool. I'd been half-asleep and standing. "Hello," I said. "Sorry, I—oh, it's you. Hi, Kayla!"

The young woman, a co-guest at the Oceanside, offered me a weary smile. "Morning," she said. "I thought it would be best to come get a cup of coffee today. I'm not huge on drinking the stuff, but goodness, after last night..."

"Totally," I said and set my cold cup down. I poured her one, slipped it into a coffee cup holder, and handed it over. "There you go."

"Thank you," Kayla said, brushing back short, dark hair from her bright green eyes. "This is terrible for my diet, but my trainer said it's good to take a break once in a while."

"Your trainer?" Bee asked as she finished serving

another customer. The line had dwindled now that the morning coffee and cake rush had ended. Likely, we'd have a few moments to ourselves until the brunch crowd rushed in.

"Oh yeah." Kayla tore the top off a pack of sugar and poured the contents into her cup. "I'm a bodybuilder."

I blinked. "You are?"

She didn't look particularly muscly, but then, who could tell? She wore a baggy shirt and a pair of jeans.

"Yes," Kayla laughed. "Priceless. I always get that reaction when I tell people. I look small, but if you had to come by the competition, you'd see just how strong I am." She set down her cup and pulled a sleeve back, showing off a bicep that was the size of my head.

Well, not quite, but it was still impressive. "You're in town for a competition?"

"That's right!" Kayla withdrew a newspaper clipping from her pocket and pointed at the headline. "See? Carmel Springs hosts the Female Bodybuilders' Association Competition." She tucked the clipping away again. "And I'm going to win. If I can get some sleep. I won't be able to train and prepare when I'm this tired."

"Ugh, that's terrible."

"But not as terrible as the fact that a man died last night," Bee said. "Don't get me wrong, I wasn't Jones's biggest fan, but what a way to go."

"Nightmarish," Kayla agreed, shuddering. "I've never seen anything like that before."

"I wish we could say the same." There had been a few incidents in the last few months, and we'd managed to get involved in all of them.

Kayla paid for her coffee then headed off toward the benches that overlooked the ocean. It was a clear day today, and the water was glassy and smooth. The wind refreshed me a little, but definitely not enough to wake me fully.

More customers arrived, seeking treats and chatter, including the Carlingtons—the elderly couple who'd been staying at the Oceanside over Halloween, and who had attended my surprise party as well. Mrs. Carlington was short and sweet as honey. She wore polka-dot dresses and could produce candies from her bag at a moment's notice. Mr. Carlington smoked a pipe and was tall and thin as a rake but was always ready with a book recommendation or an interesting fact.

"Good morning, dears," Mrs. Carlington said. "Do you have any specials this week?"

"Lemon meringue cupcakes in celebration of Ruby's birthday," Bee said, gesturing to the stacked display case behind the counter. The cupcakes were another of Bee's amazing inventions. A tangy lemon frosting, a vanilla cupcake, and zesty meringues atop it, dotted with beads of golden syrup.

"They look divine," Mrs. Carlington said. "Two please."

"Absolutely." I set to work packaging two of the cupcakes in a Bite-sized Bakery box.

"Did you hear the news about the murder?" Mr. Carlington asked, producing the newspaper from underneath his arm. "I assume Detective Martin has come by to talk to you about it?"

Bee and I frowned at each other. "No? Why would he have spoken to us?" Bee asked.

"Oh. Oh dear," Mr. Carlington said and placed the newspaper on the counter.

"You've put your foot in it again, Jeffrey."

"I have indeed," Mr. Carlington said. "Well, no harm in telling all, now, since my foot's already in the—"

"Jeffrey, please!"

"Right. Heavens, Deirdre, I wasn't going to say anything too inappropriate. I'm not that invested in toilet humor." Mr. Carlington had gone flustered and tugged on the collar of his shirt. "The newspapers have announced that Jones wasn't killed by a knife but a letter opener."

"Oh. What's that got to do with us?" I asked.

"The letter opener was from Bee's room."

Bee went wide-eyed.

I grabbed the paper, fluffing it out to read it. "It can't

say that. How could they possibly know...?" But there it was, announced plainly on the front page.

—a letter opener, taken from one of the guest's rooms. Our sources close to the scene tell us that the letter opener in question came from Beatrice Pine's suite. Could it be that the out-of-towner had taken it upon herself to—

"Drivel," Mrs. Carlington said, reaching over to pat Bee on the arm. "Don't worry yourself with that. It's second-rate journalism at best, and there's no evidence that—"

A siren whooped outside the truck, and Detective Martin's police cruiser rolled to a halt in front of the food truck. He emerged from it, settling his hat on his thatch of thick, brown hair.

"Miss Pine?" The detective stopped behind the Carlingtons. "Do you have a minute to talk to me? It's important."

Four

The day on the food truck ended earlier than usual, mostly because Bee and I were too tired to continue. Folks in Carmel Springs seemed more interested in talking about the murder than buying our cupcakes, too, and though I wasn't big on celebrating birthdays, this was hardly how I'd envisioned my week going.

"Are you OK?" I asked as we clambered into the truck —Bee in the passenger seat and me in the driver's. "I mean, Detective Martin..."

"He's just doing his job," Bee said. "What? I can be nice too. I can tell that Martin is a good officer. He's following every lead. If they had anything on me, I'd be in prison by now, but they don't, and I'm not."

"Did he let anything slip?" I started the truck, allowing

the engine to warm up. A lot of people didn't know that driving off with their engine cold could damage it—this way, I saved myself money on repairs and got time to myself. Or time with Bee to talk about the murder.

"Hmm." Bee peered out of the windshield at the ocean. The sun was now high overhead, just past its zenith. "I didn't get to press him for much information, but he did mention that he'd been busy all morning and apologized that I'd read about the letter opener in the newspaper before he'd gotten the chance to come and talk to me."

"Oh?"

"Yeah, he mentioned he'd had to calm down Jones's grieving widow." Bee rapped her knuckles absently on her window. "I wonder who she is."

"That's an easy solve," I replied, bringing out my phone and unlocking the screen. I shot off a quick text to Millie, our friend and the Queen of gossip and news in town. The reply came through seconds later, lighting my screen and sending bubbles of excitement through me. "Martha Jones. And here's her address."

"Number 22 Syrup Street," Bee read aloud. "What's with this town and the cutesy names?"

"What do you say?" I asked. "Do you want to go have a chat with the widow? Or do you want to stay out of this one?" We'd gotten involved, whether we'd meant to or not, in the last few cases in town. Cases that Jones had headed, and that he'd been protective over.

And he locked you up, remember? It's a miracle you're not a major suspect. Yet.

"I think the choice has been taken away from us," Bee said. "What are we going to do? Serve cakes while the cops look for evidence that links me to the crime?"

"I thought you said that Martin was a good detective."

"He seems like one," Bee said. "But I just … the thought of standing by while my name is on the line doesn't sit well with me." She ruffled her silver-gray bob. "It's taken me sixty years to start enjoying life. I'm not going to let fate take control now."

"Or handsome detectives," I said.

"Ha! So you do think he's handsome."

"And, that's my cue to leave," I said, letting down the handbrake and pulling out onto the street.

I entered Syrup Street five minutes later and parked outside number 22. It was a lovely neighborhood, with gorgeous trees, their leaves golden-brown and dropping from the branches. There were benches and lampposts, and the houses were neat with yards that were small but cared for.

"Nice place," I said.

"Never judge a neighborhood by its, err, cover?"

"Well put."

"I'm too tired to come up with snappy puns, but you get what I mean," Bee said, as we got out of the food truck. "There's a seedy underbelly in a lot of places that look charming and quaint."

"All right, all right, don't go all 'seedy' on me."

I opened the picket gate that let into Martha Jones's yard and made my way up the path to the front of the house. It was squat, the front porch devoid of decoration. I couldn't help but think that was the detective's doing. He'd never seemed like the type to go for anything frivolous or fun. He'd been downright nasty toward us most of the time.

Bee knocked and rang the doorbell, and we waited, the quiet broken by the odd barking of a dog or the rush of leaves skittering across the sidewalk.

The door opened, and a woman who sort of looked like Miss Piggy, if Miss Piggy had turned human, smiled out at us. "Hello," she said. "Can I help you with something?"

"Hi there," I said. "My name is Ruby Holmes, and this is—"

"Beatrice Pine." Martha, Jones's widow, opened the door wider. "You two had better come inside. Follow me." She walked down a long hall that was filled with boxes and a floral-patterned fabric bag. "In here." She paused in a doorway, beckoning to us.

Bee and I exchanged one of our "what on earth is this" glances, then followed her into the house. We entered a living room that held a set of leather sofas and a flat-screen TV on the wall, beneath the stuffed heads of two deer.

"I see you're admiring Roger and Macy," Martha said, and I startled.

"I'm sorry, who?"

"The deer." Martha busied herself moving around the living room, drawing curtains back to let in light. "They were my husband's favorites. He bagged them on a hunting trip over in Milwaukee."

"Oh." I wasn't a huge fan of hunting.

Bee sniffed. "How did you know our names?" she asked.

"Oh, Nathan talked about you two all the time. You were a thorn in his side," Martha replied. "Would you like some coffee? Tea?"

"No, thank you," I said.

We took a seat on one of the sofas, the leather squeaking beneath us.

Martha stood for a second longer, peering out the window that looked onto the street. "Nathan mentioned your food truck often too." She bent and retrieved a newspaper from next to the sofa. "And the headlines say that it was your letter opener that..." She closed her eyes for a second, trembling on the spot. "I was silly to invite you in. I was simply curious. You don't seem that bad. The way he spoke about you, I half-expected you would have horns and forked tongues."

"Sheesh," Bee said. "That's good to know."

"We're not here to cause you in any trouble, Mrs. Jones. We just wanted to offer our condolences." My gaze was drawn to the boxes out in the hall, though, a few of them visible beneath a table. They were sealed shut with tape and marked "cushions" and "books." "I see you're packing. Do you need help with anything?"

"Oh, that's so sweet of you," Martha said, her expression flickering strangely, perhaps between fear and anger and something else? "I don't understand why my husband hated you so much, but no, I don't need help. I'm going away on a little vacation, just to get some breathing room after what's happened."

A vacation that required her to pack up her house? And cushions and books?

"We have some cupcakes out in the food truck if you'd like some," Bee said. "It's the least we can do."

"No, no, that's fine. I'm fine. Or I will be fine." Martha still hadn't sat down. "I guess, it's just very strange to wake up and have the house empty of him. He wasn't the most ebullient of men, but we had been together for so long. It's just strange." She pressed a hand to her forehead, disturbing her honey-blonde fringe. "I don't think it's registered yet. I just—oh my." She finally lowered herself to the sofa, and the leather screamed a protest.

It would have been funny if not for the situation. "Mrs. Jones, is there anything we can do? Anything at all?" I asked.

"No," Martha said. "No, I think I need to be alone now. Thank you for offering your condolences. I appreciate it."

Bee and I filed out of the house as quietly as we'd come, past the boxes that surely shouldn't have been there if Martha was just "going on vacation."

"What do you think?" I asked, after we'd slipped into the truck and fastened our seatbelts.

"That Martha's got something to hide. Why else would she have lied to us about going away?" Bee replied. "I'm sorry, but there's no way what's going on in there qualifies as 'packing for a vacation.' The whole thing felt weird. Especially with the two deer watching us."

"Eugh." I stuck out my tongue. "That was strange." And it was even weirder to picture Martha and Jones as a married couple. I hadn't bothered wondering if he had a significant other. I'd assumed that no woman would be able to tolerate his ego.

Boy, had I been wrong.

"Let's go, Rubes. We should take it easy tonight. We'll need our wits about us tomorrow."

"And the day after that." Depending on how long the case lasted, of course.

It was time to put our sleuthing caps on again.

Five

It had taken two days for the police to clear the guesthouse of evidence, the body, and the crime scene tape, but we were finally back. Strangely, the Oceanside felt more like home to me now than my apartment back in New York ever had. At least, here we could get some proper sleep.

Assuming Jones didn't decide to come back and haunt our rooms. He had truly despised us, Bee in particular. I wouldn't have put it past him to use his afterlife to punish us for our past transgressions.

I sat at our favorite table in the living room, the one closest to the fireplace, a cup of coffee in front of me. Bee read a newspaper from a day prior to the murder—Sam hadn't had a chance to bring in the latest, and we were both too lazy to go out and get it.

"It's good to be back." I took a sip of my coffee, scanning the room. The chairs and tables were back in their usual arrangement. The gifts that I'd been bought had been confiscated, and a few of them had been ruined because of Jones's weight.

Terrible thought. Poor guy. Was it disingenuous of me to feel pity for Jones? He'd been an enemy of mine, in a way, but I would never have wished death upon him. Or anything bad for that matter. All I'd wanted was for him to leave me alone.

The Carlingtons sat at their favorite spot next to the window, occasionally chatting or sipping from their mugs, while Trouble the kitten lay in front of the fireplace, warming his fluffy underbelly.

"That's interesting," Bee said, turning the pages of the paper.

"What is?"

"This." She pressed the newspaper flat to the table. "There's an op-ed piece in here from Millie. It was written the day before Jones's murder."

"Oh? What does it say?"

Bee read in hushed tones, her fingers crinkling the paper. "It is the opinion of the editor that the police department in Carmel Springs is in serious need of assistance and perhaps a change in management. Too often are officers like Detective Nathan Jones allowed to run amok, arresting innocents or making unfounded accusations. If these sorts of instances don't come to an end, there will only be pain, confusion, and upset in the future."

I sat back. "Wow. Sounds like Millie wasn't Jones's biggest fan either."

"Hmm."

"What?"

"Did you see her yesterday?"

"Yesterday? Where?"

Bee folded the old newspaper and placed it to one side. "On the food truck. Did you serve her?"

"No. I haven't served her since ... the day of the murder, I think. My birthday."

"And neither have I." Bee pursed her lips. "Millie never misses a chance to gossip and have a cupcake. It's weird that she wouldn't have come by to talk about Jones's death."

"You can't possibly think that she would do anything like that. Come on, Bee, we know Millie. She's a good person. She was the one who helped us drum up interest for the truck a few weeks ago," I said.

"Yes, yes, I know. But if we're going to figure out who did this, we have to make sure that we investigate every possible avenue. We can't be biased. It seems to me that Millie might have a reason to stay away. Maybe she's afraid we saw the article. Maybe she thinks that we'll ask her questions about it."

"I don't know."

"If she had something to hide, she'd stay away."

"She's probably been busy," I replied. "We can't just assume that it's got to do with the murder."

Bee shrugged. "It's strange, though, that she's avoiding the truck days after Jones was murdered, and after she wrote this article about him. Just saying."

I opened my mouth to argue Bee down from the mystery ledge, but Sam emerged from the kitchen carrying two plates with our breakfasts. She set them down in front us—a croissant with strawberry preserves for me, and a plate of scrambled eggs and bacon for Bee, syrup on the side in case she wanted it.

"Thanks, Sam," I said. "This smells delicious. Um, but could I perhaps get that cheese we talked about?"

"Right! Right, of course. Sorry, Ruby. Sorry." Sam jerked on the spot as if I'd screamed at her then rushed back into the kitchen.

"She's jumpy," Bee whispered.

I nodded. But suspecting Sam of murder was even more ridiculous than the thought of Millie attacking Jones with a letter opener. She was our friend and a bit of a pushover.

Sam entered the dining area carrying a small ramekin

of grated cheddar and put it next to my plate. "There you go. It's my fault. I forgot to tell Shawn you wanted the cheese."

Shawn was Sam's newest assistant—a young man who'd once been on Jones's suspect list for murder. He'd done nothing but cook delicious meals since Sam had hired him, though, and hadn't done anything remotely illegal either.

"Are you all right?" Bee asked as she crunched on a piece of crispy bacon. "You're pale."

"I'm fine," she said. "I guess it was the stress of what happened. I can't believe that my guesthouse was the site of a m-murder."

"It's terrible. But don't worry, Sam, they'll catch who did this."

If anything, Sam only grew paler. "Yes. That's good. I want Carmel Springs to be safe again."

"So do we," I said. "Especially since we've decided we're staying for Christmas."

"That's wonderful," Sam replied, absently.

"Say, Sam." Bee paused her crunching. "I'm curious, did you see anything strange on the night of the murder?"

Again, Sam jumped on the spot. "The m-murder? No. Why? What do you mean?"

Goodness, she was acting different. I cleared my throat. "I think Bee's asking if you saw anyone around the guesthouse. You know, someone who maybe didn't belong or who might have been snooping around upstairs."

"Upstairs, yeah," Bee said. "They took my letter opener to kill Jones. So it might have been someone trying to frame me. Someone who hated Jones and maybe hated me too."

Sam appeared frozen, a deer in headlights.

"Sam?"

"No," she said, jerking her head from side-to-side. "No, I didn't see anything. Now, if you'll excuse me, I've got to go, um, go check on Shawn. See if he needs any help with the other breakfasts." She hurried back into the kitchen, the doors swinging shut behind her.

Bee and I raised our eyebrows at each other.

"What was that about?" I asked.

"I don't know. But I have a feeling we're going to find out. Sooner rather than later."

Six

THE SUN HAD DIPPED TOWARD THE HORIZON, and we were at the end of another day on the food truck. Business had been better today and easier since we weren't both exhausted and overwrought from the "excitement" surrounding Jones's untimely demise. But I couldn't quit thinking about Sam.

Why had she been so jumpy this morning? What had gotten into her? Was it because of the scare of seeing Jones's body? Or was there more to it than that?

You can't seriously suspect that Sam had anything to do with it. She's a lovely person.

"What a day," Bee said, as she clambered into the passenger seat of the truck. "That Kayla sure can eat. She bought an entire box of dusted donuts this morning and devoured them at one of the beachside benches." She lifted a finger. "In one sitting. That's no mean feat. Take it from someone who loves donuts as much as I do."

"Doesn't seem like the prime bodybuilder diet to me. But what do I know?"

"How to make a donut," Bee said.

"And that's thanks to you." I'd slowly started learning how to create baked goods since we'd started our adventure together. It was heartening to have Bee by my side, guiding me through the process and pointing out when I'd made a mistake, usually with a chuckle.

We drove down the road toward the Oceanside, past the quaint houses, the pier, and the Lobster Shack—we'd have to visit it again now that it had reopened. Finally, we parked in front of the guesthouse. The engine ticked as it cooled.

I was so ready for a long hot bath and one of Shawn's delicious dinners—who would have thought that a troubled young man like him would have such a knack for cooking? It was more evidence that one simply couldn't judge a book by its cover.

"Uh oh."

"What?" I asked.

"Look." Bee pointed at the guesthouse.

On the front porch, Detective Martin stood with his

notepad out in deep discussion with Shawn. The youngster kept flipping his dark hair back, a scowl parting his lips. He shook his head, denying whatever Detective Martin had said.

"What do you think that's about?" I asked.

"I think we both know. The murder. Maybe Martin thinks that Shawn had something to do with it."

"Surely not. Shawn's got his history, but he'd not a bad guy."

"No, he's not," Bee said firmly.

In the short while since Shawn had started working at the guesthouse, he and Bee had forged an easy friendship. It was probably because they both liked their privacy, and because during Bee's fluey stint, Shawn had snuck her some pancakes when Sam wasn't looking. Sam had ordained that Bee should be fed chicken soup only.

Detective Martin capped his pen, put his notepad away, then drew a card from his pocket and gave it to Shawn. Finally, he walked down the steps and toward his cruiser. He either didn't notice us or didn't bother greeting, which suited me just fine. Handsome or not, there was more chance of me growing a fluffy tail and becoming the Easter Bunny than there was I'd ever date again.

And particularly not a gorgeous detective who smelled of sandalwood. *Oof, stop that!*

"Come on," Bee said. "Let's find out what happened."

We met Shawn on the porch. The Oceanside's new chef stared at the card the detective had given him.

"Evening, Shawn," Bee said.

He shifted and tucked the card into his pocket. "Hi. We're having lobster ravioli for dinner."

"That's great!" My stomach growled loudly in agreement. "But actually, we were just wondering what that was about."

"The detective?" Shawn rolled his eyes. "He wanted to talk to me about Jones's death. Thinks I might have had something to do with it. You know, because I'm such a good scapegoat. Man, I ain't done nothing wrong in weeks, and now this happens, and I'm back on the radar. It's dumb." He scuffed his thick-soled boot on the porch boards.

"I happen to agree with you," Bee said.

"Look, Shawn, we're going to be, well, checking out a few leads and clues ourselves. We don't think you did it—"

"No one who cooks as well as you do could be a murderer," Bee interjected.

"But we want to find out who did. Is there any reason Detective Martin might suspect you were involved?"

Shawn scratched the back of his neck. "Well, yeah, I can understand why. It was this thing that happened a little while ago. Like maybe, I dunno, three or four days before someone offed the guy."

"What happened?" I asked.

"I was in the Corner Café grabbing a coffee. They got nice coffee. I like it because they've got all types, and I wanted to try their new cappuccino."

"Ooh, the pumpkin spice?" Bee asked.

"Yeah, yeah, that one!" Shawn lit up at the memory, but his brow wrinkled right afterward. "And then Jones came in, probably for his coffee too. But he couldn't just leave me alone. He caused a scene, started making a big deal out of the fact that I was in there."

"What did he say?"

"That I was a good-for-nothing and that I was a danger to society or whatever. A lot of people stared or grumbled, but nobody said a thing about it. They were all too afraid of him, because he could put them away, I guess. He said that I shouldn't come back to the Corner Café ever again because it wasn't for deadbeats and that if I did, he'd take everything away from me."

"Wow," I said. "Wow, that's crazy."

"That sounds like Detective Jones to me," Bee put in. "The man had a screw loose. Not to speak ill of the dead or anything, but he wasn't all there. He arrested Ruby for no good reason after Theresa Michaud was murdered."

"Oh yeah, I remember," Shawn said. "Anyway, now,

because of that, and everybody saw it too, that Detective Martin's all over me. Asking questions and wanting alibis and all that. It's annoying. I was at the guesthouse with everybody else during the build-up to the surprise party. And I didn't kill Jones. He wasn't worth my time." He fiddled with the pocket of his Oceanside Guesthouse apron. "Man, why would I mess everything up like that? And a letter opener? Who stabs somebody with a letter opener? It's just weird."

"Agreed." Bee and I linked arms and followed Shawn back into the guesthouse. The scents of lobster ravioli were already on the air. I couldn't wait to freshen up and tuck into Shawn's latest creation, but the worry over the case stuck with me.

Now, we had several suspects, and all of them were either friends or folks we thought couldn't possibly commit the murder. Sam, Millie, and Shawn. But their connections to Jones's death were tenuous at best.

"What do you think?" I asked Bee.

She stopped in front of the stairs, peering up at the landing. The doorway to her room and mine were the first and second ones on the right. "I don't know. But I'm wondering if they were out to get me or Jones. Why did they have the letter opener from my room?"

If only I'd had an answer. "I think we should check out the Corner Café," I said, "and talk to a few of the people or servers there. See if they maybe heard something. Shawn could be lying."

"True. He could be. But I doubt it. That young man isn't the most orthodox in style or behavior, but I wouldn't peg him as a murderer."

"There's only one way we'll find out."

Seven

"So, what are our options?" Bee asked, rubbing her palms together.

We'd taken the window seat in the Corner Café, which looked out on the town hall and the activity in Main Street. More of those wrought-iron lamps populated the neat sidewalk, along with benches, a bus stop, and neatly demarcated parking spaces. Folks walked along, stopping at stores for what they needed or chatting with friends.

The view was gorgeous, and the scents of roasting coffee beans and fresh-baked muffins and croissants uplifted me. And made me hungry. I scanned my menu, picking out a worthy brunch.

The Eggs Benedict looked amazing. Or a muffin.

"We could talk to our server, see if maybe he was on

duty," I said. "Or, wait, didn't Shawn say that he was here to get a coffee?"

"Pumpkin spice cappuccino," Bee said, tapping on the menu card in front of her. "I'm dying for one of them."

"Not dying, I hope."

"Very funny."

"I try," I said, scanning the place. "The barista. That's it. We should talk to the barista. From the sounds of it, Shawn was in the line when Jones came in and confronted him. So it's most likely that the barista would've seen it all."

"Hmm, assuming it's the same barista on duty today," Bee put in. "We could possibly…" Bee went quiet, her mouth hanging open.

"Possibly what?" I frowned.

Bee stared over my shoulder, at the doorway to the Corner Café.

"Bee?"

"Shush," she hissed. "Just a second. Act natural."

"I'm not the one behaving strangely."

"Yes, yes. Hmm. Pretend we're talking about something and don't look," Bee said.

"Firstly, we are talking about something, unless we've entered another dimension where moving one's mouth and tongue and forming actual words doesn't count as speech, and secondly—"

"It's Millie," Bee whispered.

I stopped talking, instantly.

"No, no, not like that. You have to talk, or she might look up and see us and think we're staring at her."

It took all my focus and determination not to turn in my seat and look over at the point that had so fixated Bee. "OK, um, tell me what's going on. What is she doing? Who is she with?"

"Just a second." Bee lifted her menu card and held it near her face, switching her gaze from it to the table where Millie was obviously seated. Not that I could tell without giving the whole game away.

"Well?"

"She's pale and hunching over. She's lifting her menu. Her fingers are trembling like, like... um... like a—"

"Is the metaphor really important?" I asked.

"I suppose it isn't," she replied. "She's with a man. A stranger. Never seen him near the food truck, and he doesn't look friendly either."

"I have to see this."

"Don't you dare turn around! You'll give up our position."

"Relax, Bee. We're not undercover cops." I rose from the table and walked to the front of the coffee shop, joining the queue that wound from the counter backward.

This was our chance to figure out exactly what Millie was up to.

Casually, I removed my phone from my pocket and turned sideways, pretending to be engrossed in a game or a message from a friend. My gaze lifted, slowly, and I spotted Millie sitting at a table against the wall. She had tied back her gray hair in a severe bun—not like her at all—and wore no makeup. She'd also dressed in baggier clothes than usual—shapeless pants and a shirt that hung low.

What on earth? How strange.

The man seated across from her was tan with an aquiline nose and sharp green eyes. They flashed as he spoke, seemingly under his breath, leaning toward Millie. She sat deathly still, staring at him, unspeaking.

What is that about?

Millie was usually such a light, friendly person. She'd always had time to chat with us. She'd helped us with our—

"Excuse me," a woman said, loudly.

I jumped and threw my phone upward. It turned end-over-end and careened toward the floor. I stuck out my hand and caught it, but it slipped and fell into the other, and I proceeded to juggle it on the spot and force it toward my chest. I pinned it against my shirt with my forearm.

Everyone in the Corner Café turned their heads.

"Sorry," I said.

But it was too late. Millie had spotted me. She paled and leaned in, hurriedly. She whispered something, and both she and the mystery man got up and exited the establishment.

"Excuse me." The woman behind me in the line pursed her lips. "Like, some of us need our coffee fix. Can you move it along?"

In my quest to spy on Millie, I'd failed to notice that the line had shifted forward. "Right, sorry." I scurried up to the counter. "Hi," I said, to the barista, barely keeping track of my words. "Um, can I get two pumpkin spice cappuccinos please?"

"Sure."

Bee joined me and nudged me in the ribs. "You should take up a job in the FBI," she said. "You'd be great at blending in."

"It was an accident."

"Is that what that was? It looked like you'd decided to take up juggling and missed all your practice sessions."

"Now, who should be a comedian?" I asked.

We got our cappuccinos and proceeded back to our spot in front of the window. I sat down and inhaled the delicious scent of the coffee, the aroma invigorating me. "Shoot. I forgot to ask the barista about Shawn and Jones."

"Forget them," Bee said, waving a hand. "What about

Millie? Did you see how she jumped? The minute she saw you, she went pale as flour and ran out of here.”

“I saw.”

“She’s avoiding us,” Bee declared. “But why? What could she be up to? And who was that guy?”

“I don’t know. And I’m not sure how comfortable I feel about prying into her life. It seems wrong. Millie’s been nothing but kind to us, and I just don’t see her being the murdering type.” I’d said “murdering” a little too loud, and the lady at the table behind us gasped. “Sorry,” I said. “Just, um, gossiping about the news.”

The woman exhaled and nodded in apparent relief. Because gossiping about murder was normal, apparently.

“Sure, Millie doesn’t seem like the murdering type,” Bee said, measuring her tone better than I’d done. “But what about the guy that was with her? He looked like... like... Al Capone.”

“But thinner. And with a sharper nose.”

“Exactly.” Bee mixed sugar into her coffee with a stirring stick. “Point is, he looked more than capable of, you know, offing a fool.”

“Since when do you speak mafia?”

Bee rolled her eyes. “Come on, we’ve got to find out who he is. Somebody has to know something.”

“Bee, we’ve taken more than enough time off today. We need to get out on the truck and focus on our real jobs.

Baking and making people happy. Not investigating our friend," I said.

"Bah, humbug." Bee knew I was right, though.

We finished our delicious cappuccinos in silence, both transfixed by the passing cars and people. My thoughts were on Millie and the strange man. He'd definitely looked ... like he was from out-of-town. Rich coming from me, sure, but true.

Why was Millie spending time with him?

And what business did he have in Carmel Springs?

Not my business. Not my business at all.

Eight

BUSINESS ON THE FOOD TRUCK WAS BETTER THAN ever. Folks lined up in front of it, hungry for the special lemon meringue cupcakes and a new number Bee had whipped up: the pumpkin spice cookie to be served with our pumpkin spice lattes. Thanksgiving was on the horizon, and people were ready to celebrate it.

"These are delicious," a customer said, lifting a cookie. "I can't get enough of them. Can I get ten to go? My kids will love them too."

"Of course," I said and busied myself preparing the order and ringing it up on the cash register.

Usually, the days on the truck were punctuated by chatter, laughter, and the view of the ocean, the sunlight glimmering on the waves. But today was different—storm clouds gathered in the distance, and I couldn't help but think they were an omen of sorts.

What had Millie been doing with that strange man?

I'd insisted on ignoring her meeting with him and focusing on the food truck, instead, but now that I was here, I couldn't stop myself from pondering the possibilities. What if he was some kind of Mafioso? Could Millie really be involved in Detective Jones's death?

Ooh, what if Millie was being blackmailed by the mafia man? She might have seen something, and now he was after her to shut her trap. She could be in danger!

Ridiculous, you don't even know who the guy is. He's probably not a mafia guy.

"Good afternoon, Kayla," Bee said.

Our co-guest in the Oceanside stepped up, looking beefier than usual. That might've been because she'd spent the last few mornings shoveling back donuts, cupcakes, and treats.

"Hello," she said and offered both of us a smile. "I've come for sustenance. I've got to eat if I want to stay big for the competition."

I tucked hands into the front pocket of my apron. "Of course! When is it? And are you supposed to be eating so many sweet treats before it starts?"

"I look good no matter what I eat," Kayla said, lifting her chin. "I work out all day, apart from when I'm eating, so yeah, why not treat myself? And the competition's next week. I'm really nervous about it, but shoot, I know I'll win. No amount of sweet treats will stop me. Besides, it's sustenance, and there are loads of good fats in here."

Was there much competition for bodybuilding females in Maine? Regardless, she had a goal, and I was all for a woman who took control of her own destiny. "We'll be rooting for you. We could come by and give a few cheers, you know."

"No, that's fine. You don't have to come. It will just be a whole bunch of us posing for judges," Kayla said, quickly.

"What can we get for you today, Kayla?" Bee asked, clearly as eager to return to her own thoughts and ponderings as I was. Maybe she'd developed a few more theories about who the stranger had been. Or she'd suggest we go find out by confronting him. Definitely not a wise idea.

"Give me a dozen of those pumpkin spice cookies, please. And a soda. I want something cold to wash the goodness down. Oh, but make it a diet soda, please."

"Will do," Bee said and set to work packaging and pouring.

"Coming to this food truck is a highlight of my day," Kayla said, while she waited. "And the bonus is I get to leave the guesthouse."

"You don't like it there?" I asked. "Did the murder creep you out?" It had bothered all of us.

"Well, kinda, but that's not why I don't like being there. I don't' want to run into…" she trailed off, glancing over her shoulder to check no one was within earshot. She licked her lips. "Can you guys keep a secret?"

"Sure can," I said.

Bee snorted.

"I mean, it's not that big of a deal. It's just a rumor I heard. And it's put me on edge. Like … why would she have done that?"

"Done what?" I asked, leaning my hands on the countertop.

Bee had stopped feeding cookies into a candy-striped box, her focus on Kayla, as well.

The bodybuilder ruffled her short black hair and drew closer. "Well, I was talking to Mrs. Carlington yesterday afternoon at lunchtime, and apparently, she and Mr. Carlington saw Sam snooping around Detective Jones's house the night before the murder."

The information didn't compute for a moment. "Sam? Snooping?" It didn't seem plausible. Why would Sam have been snooping around the detective's house?

I think you know why.

But no, I couldn't believe that Sam had darkness in her heart. Surely not.

"She was snooping?" Bee asked.

"Yeah. Apparently, the Carlingtons were on their way home from a restaurant, and they saw her. In the front garden. Peering through the windows."

That didn't' sound good.

"Wow," I said. "Are you sure?"

"You can ask them if you'd like. I wasn't the one who saw it. Can I get my cookies now?"

"Right." Bee finished up and handed the box over then the soda too. She rang up the order and tendered the change. "Enjoy them."

"Thanks. You guys be safe. I don't know how I feel about being in the guesthouse at the moment. What if Sam was the one who ... you know. Did it. Like, she seems so nice, but you can never tell, can you? It's often the nice ones who are mean deep down." And she marched off and took a place at one of the benches. She popped the box open and set to work, shoving cookies into her mouth.

"This can't be true," I said.

"Like she said, we can ask the Carlingtons. They have no reason to lie."

"Unless they were the ones who did it."

Bee raised a silver eyebrow at me. "Come on, Rubes, you and I both know those two aren't energetic enough to drag a body around in a guesthouse. They're ancient."

"They're only five years older than you."

"Age is just a number. But fitness is underrated. I go jogging. I doubt either of them is into anything particularly strenuous."

"It's ironic that you're an ageist," I said.

"Fitness snob, more like."

I brought out a dish towel and cleaned off the counter, even though there was nothing on it that needed cleaning. "Do you believe it?" I asked. "That Sam was snooping around in Jones's front garden?"

"I don't know. Maybe. But there's only one way we can know for sure, and that's by asking her."

My belly flipped, flopped, and wiggled like a fish out of water. I was used to talking to people, confronting them even, but doing it to Sam would be so weird. She was such a good friend now, and if she thought that we were accusing he,r it would ruin what we'd built up.

"I know what you're thinking," Bee said, "but we can easily phrase it as us trying to clear her name, rather than thinking she'd done something wrong."

"I just don't want this to ruin Thanksgiving. Or Christmas. I don't want Sam to get in trouble either."

"She won't get into trouble if she hasn't done anything wrong," Bee said.

She had a point there. And as far as I was concerned, there wasn't a chance that Sam had actually murdered

Detective Jones. In fact, there was more chance of the sky turning purple and Santa Claus descending on the food truck with a bag full of coal.

"All right," I said. "Let's talk to her."

Nine

The guesthouse's dining area was empty, the clock on the wall ticking gently and displaying the time as six pm. It was just past dinnertime, and the meals had all been cleared away. The other guests had returned to their rooms, all except for Bee and me.

My stomach ached. I'd hardly eaten a bite of the sumptuous lobster mac and cheese that Shawn had prepared for us because I'd been too nervous. It was time to talk to her about the rumors floating around in town.

It wasn't that I thought she'd actually done it. No, that simply couldn't be true. I just didn't want to lose her as a friend for asking. And it was necessary to clear every possible suspect so we could find the real killer.

Bee sat near the fire, logs crackling merrily in the grate, and I held Trouble in my lap, stroking his fluffy ears.

The kitchen doors opened, and Sam came out into the living room, brushing off her shirt. She spotted us and jerked as if she'd been electrified. "Oh! Sorry, I thought everyone had already gone up to bed."

"Not everyone," Bee said and folded her newspaper. "Good evening, Samantha."

I frowned at Bee. She'd sounded a little too interrogatory, even in her greeting. "Could we talk to you for a second, Sam?" I asked.

She chewed on her lip, her shoulders rising.

"Sam?"

"So you heard," she said.

"Heard what?" I asked.

Sam stood silent then came forward and lowered herself into one of the armchairs near the fire, the light casting flickering shadows along the side of her pale face. "About Detective Martin coming around to ask me questions. I've been so stressed about it. Terrified that everyone in town will hear about i, and think that I was involved somehow, and then the guesthouse..." She hung her head. "I've worked for years to try make this place better. I just ... I want everything to work out. And now Detective Jones has been murdered, and right here. Right here."

"It's OK, Sam," I said.

"Not really," said Bee.

Sam's head came up, and I swiveled toward Bee. "Is it necessary to be like that?" I asked.

"Yes," Bee said, firmly. "Now, Sam, we love you to pieces. We think you're an amazing person, but if you want us to help you prove that it wasn't you who killed Detective Jones, you're going to have to hold your head up higher and act a little stronger."

Tears glistened on Sam's eyelashes. "What do you mean?"

"She means that we need you to help us help you."

"But how?" Sam asked. Trouble meowed and hopped from my lap to hers, turning in a quick circle and kneading her jeans.

"By telling us the truth," Bee said. "We heard that you were snooping around Detective Jones's house a few days before he was murdered. We want to know why."

Sam's bottom lip trembled. Trouble lifted his kitty head and meowed at her. It was amazing how animals could pick up on distress, and even more amazing how terrible I felt about the questions we had to ask. This was why I could never be a police officer. Separating my emotions from a case seemed nearly impossible.

Luckily, Bee was stone-cold. She was the one who did most of the unemotional, logical reasoning.

"Sam?" Bee asked.

She let out a long, low breath. "That's what everyone

thinks?" she asked. "That I was snooping around because I wanted to kill Jones?"

"Not necessarily," I said. "But you can see how it's suspicious. Maybe if you just told us why…"

"I feel like I can't," Sam whispered. "It's not my place to say anything."

"Sam, you realize that this is looking pretty bad for you. Better you break someone's trust than wind up in prison for a crime you didn't commit," Bee said, sharply.

Again, Sam went all wobbly-lipped. "I was there looking for Martha."

"Martha? Jones's wife?"

"That's right," she said. "I've been friends with her for a while, and she needed my help."

"With what?" Bee asked. "And why would she need your help so late at night?"

"Because she was looking to divorce Jones, and she didn't want anyone to know, and she wanted to try a trial separation, and—"

"Whoa." I raised my hand. "Slow down, Sam. Can you start from the beginning?"

Samantha nodded. "Right, well, Martha came to me a few weeks ago and told me that she wasn't happy in her marriage. She was my mother's friend, and that sort of transferred onto me. The friendship, I mean. She wanted to try a separation because she couldn't stand Jones a second longer."

"Did she say why?" Bee asked.

"He was a tyrant at home. Always grumpy and critical. Basically, the same way he acts around town," Sam said. "Or acted. Oh heavens, I can't believe he's dead."

"Back to Martha," Bee prompted.

"Right, well, she wanted my help. She asked if she could come stay at the guesthouse for a while. She wanted to hide out before leaving Carmel Springs. And she needed help moving her things into storage too," Sam said.

"But that doesn't quite explain why you'd be snooping outside her house." Bee's tone remained sharp. I shot a look her way, but she ignored it.

"I hadn't heard from her in two days. She was supposed to be coming to the guesthouse that night, but she hadn't turned up, and she wasn't answering her phone. I was worried, so I went over there to check she was doing all right. I swear that was it. There was nothing sinister about it."

"And did you manage to get hold of her?" Bee asked.

"Yeah. She told me not to worry and that she needed a few more days to get her affairs in order." Sam stroked Trouble, her fingers worrying his fur until he caught them with his little claws and got her to stop. "I don't want to cause any trouble. For Martha or for me."

I chewed on the inside of my cheek, drawn to the flickering flames in the fireplace. Sam was stressed, clearly, and it would be easy enough to check if what she'd told us was true. We had to talk to Martha again.

And find out why she'd lied to us about her "vacation." Now that Jones was dead, why would she lie about their separation?

Because she has something else to hide.

Ten

"WE SHOULD HAVE SEEN THIS COMING." BEE LED
the charge down the sidewalk on Syrup Street. "The
spouse is always the first suspect in a murder case. People
are often motivated by anger or love or lust or revenge,
especially when it comes to their significant others."

"But that might just be us jumping to conclusions," I
said. "There might be another reason that Martha lied."

"Like what?" Bee asked. "Why would she hide what
her true intentions were? She's scared of being found out,
and that means she has a secret. Probably a dark one."

I sighed. It was troublesome to get Bee to relax once
she was on a roll, and she was surely on one now. Still, it
was a nice thought, believing that we could solve the case
as easy as that. But I doubted it—wouldn't Detective
Martin have investigated this avenue already?

"Almost there," Bee said.

Martha's neat little house was bathed in the orange glow of the setting sun, the white walls clean, the windows tightly shut against the coming of winter. Her curtains were open, though, and a TV flashed blue light in the living room. She was home.

"Are we sure about this?" I asked. "We probably shouldn't accuse her of anything." And it was sad that she'd wanted to leave Jones and had hidden it. *Unless she was hiding it because she planned on killing him.* But then why would she have told Samantha?

Bee opened the picket gate, and we hurried up the path and onto the porch. Bee knocked, and I tucked my coat against my chest, holding it tight and hoping that we didn't get in trouble for this one.

Jones is gone. Martin won't throw you in prison. But I didn't know that for sure.

The latch clicked, and Martha opened the door. Her blonde hair was done up in rollers. She snorted through her slightly upturned nose. "What are you two doing here?"

"We're sorry to bother you," I started. "But we just wanted to—"

"You lied to us," Bee said.

I stepped on the toe of her boot. She had to rein it in. For heaven's sake, we couldn't go around accusing people of murder. "What Bee means is that ... uh, yeah, basically that you didn't tell us the truth." There wasn't another way of wording it. "We talked to Sam, and she mentioned that you wanted to separate from Detective Jones. You're not going on vacation at all."

"Vacation and separation are basically the same things," Martha said, waving a hand. "And you have some kind of nerve coming over here telling me I'm a liar. What are you insinuating?"

"We're not insinuating anything," Bee said. "We're being direct. Why did you lie to us?"

"I don't have to tell you anything I don't want to," Martha replied, inching the door closed. "You're not police officers. I don't need to give you an alibi or a reason for what I do."

"We're concerned citizens," I said. "We want to help keep Carmel Springs safe. There's a murderer on the loose, and solving the crime—"

"Is not your job," Martha snapped. "At all. You're bakers. And you've overstayed your welcome."

"You can't leave." Bee folded her arms. "The police would want you to hang around until they've caught the killer."

"Is that what you think?" Martha smirked, lifting her chin. "I've already had my interview with Detective Martin, and he knows I have a rock-solid alibi, which he's confirmed, for the night of the murder. I'm free to leave Carmel Springs as soon as Nathan's last affairs have been sorted out. It wasn't me."

"Oh." Now, that did present a problem. And made us look terrible for coming over and accusing her like this.

"Oh," Bee echoed. "Well, sorry for being confrontational. We're trying to do what's right." Bee hardly every apologized unless she was sure she'd done something wrong.

"Yes, sorry," I said, blushing.

"I don't accept your apology. I don't know who you two think you are, but it's no small wonder Nathan thought you were idiots. He told me daily what trouble you had caused him. He was up at night with ulcers over it. You should be ashamed of yourselves."

Bee kept her silence.

I cleared my throat. "We haven't been going out of our way to cause trouble. We're trying to help."

"You're a hindrance," Martha said. "A waste of time. Two old women who can't control their urges to interfere. Grow up, will you?" She slapped the door shut in our faces.

It was mortifying. Absolutely humiliating, and I pressed a palm to my face, shaking my head. What made this even worse was I could understand what it was like to want to escape a town and all the memories it held. I had done the same with Daniel. Or after Daniel had disappeared.

"Stop it," Bee said, placing a hand on my shoulder. "You're being too hard on yourself. I can see it in your posture, Rubes. Don't listen to her. We've done some silly things, yes, but we've only been trying to help. And it's not our fault that the murderer decided to do the deed in the guesthouse. At your birthday party. For heaven's sake."

"Let's just go," I said.

We hurried back down the path and onto the sidewalk. I didn't look back. Martha clearly wasn't the one who'd done it, or Detective Martin wouldn't have given her permission to leave. Unless she was lying about that like she'd lied about going on vacation the other day.

"She got hostile very quickly," Bee said. "And she didn't seem that upset about the death of her husband."

"She wanted to divorce him."

"Yeah, but still. That's a person she spent most of her life with. How could she be over his death so quickly?"

I didn't have any answers.

Eleven

The purple of dusk had arrived as we turned the corner into the street that held the Oceanside. My feet were sore, my head hurt, and I was in need of a bubble bath, a cup of cocoa, and a night alone with my feet up and a good book. Perhaps something Christmas-themed to take my mind off the murder.

"I can't wait until this is over," I said. "The investigation, I mean."

"Let's hope it ends the way we want it to."

"What do you mean?"

"With the real killer behind bars, and the—" Bee stopped dead in her tracks and placed a hand on my arm. She squeezed. "Oh no."

I followed her line of sight and grew dizzy, the view of the guesthouse, with its pleasant atmosphere, warm firelight flickering in the living room windows, was marred by the police cruiser out front. Its blue-and-red lights ticked and flashed. No siren.

"What's going on?" I asked.

Another cruiser skidded around the corner, rubber squealing, and acrid smoke filled the air. It pulled into a spot next to the food truck. Two police officers jumped out, drawing their weapons.

"What is this?" I made to step forward, but Bee held me back, digging her fingernails into my arm.

"Don't interfere."

"Why not? What's happening?"

"I don't know, but you can't get in the way. You might get arrested for it, or get hurt. Those men are tense. Look at the way they're holding their guns."

"But—"

The front door of the guesthouse banged open, and Detective Martin emerged, clasping Samantha by the upper arm. He spoke quickly to her, though his words were lost in the wind.

Samantha's hands were cuffed behind her back. Tears streamed down her face. She shook her head every few minutes, her mouth moving.

"They're arresting Sam?" The words didn't fit in my mouth properly. They didn't belong.

The police officers lowered their guns and holstered

them. They came around to help Detective Martin with Samantha and placed her in the back of one of the police cars.

"What's the meaning of this?" Bee asked, storming toward Martin now the cops had stowed their weapons. "Excuse me! Detective Martin."

The detective lifted his gaze from the cruiser. He frowned at us and placed his fists on his hips. "Ladies, this is none of your business."

"Why are you arresting Samantha?" I asked.

"Because she's being arraigned for the murder of Nathan Jones."

It had been a stupid question to ask with an obvious answer, but I'd needed to hear it for myself. It was as unbelievable as I'd expected. "No," I said. "That's not possible. Samantha wouldn't hurt a fly."

Poor Sam sat in the back of the police car, tears streaking her cheeks and dropping to her lap. She wore the Oceanside Guesthouse apron, flour spattered across its front.

"She's innocent," I insisted.

"That's not for you to decide," Detective Martin replied, evenly. "We've got solid evidence that connects Samantha to the scene of the crime."

"What evidence?" Bee asked.

"That's none of your business."

"Detective Martin, please." I wasn't one for pleading, but I clasped my palms together now. "Please, you have to tell us. I simply can't believe that Samantha would—"

"Her fingerprints were on the murder weapon," Martin said, his tone gruff. "And that's the most you'll get out of me. Now, you'll have to wait until a judge sets bail if he decides she's not a flight risk, and then you can talk to her yourself. For now, stay out of trouble." He wasn't mean about it. Rather, he was professional.

I still despised it.

Bee and I retreated to the front porch, watching as the cruisers drove off with Sam.

I'd never been so low, my insides leaden with anger and frustration and guilt. If we'd figured out who'd done this sooner, Sam wouldn't be in trouble. "It can't be her," I said. "She wouldn't have hurt him. She wouldn't hurt anyone."

Trouble the kitty cat poked his head out of the still-open front door and meowed.

"Oh, poor, Trouble." I swept him into my arms and stroked his head. "It's OK, kitty. We're going to get her out of there. There's just no way she did this."

"She didn't have an alibi," Bee said. "And her fingerprints were on the letter opener. She had a motive because of Jones's past fumbling at the Oceanside. And because she was friends with Martha and was seen snooping outside her house.”

“Are you seriously telling me you believe Sam is capable of this?”

“People are capable of horrible things. Even the nicest people.” Bee scratched Trouble behind the ears, wriggling her nose from side-to-side. “But no, I don’t think Samantha did this. I don’t know what evidence the cops have, but I don’t buy it. There’s something weird going on here.”

“We have to find the murderer.”

“We will,” Bee said. “But where do we start?”

“The leads we have. There’s Shawn and Sam and Millie. The strange mafia-looking guy she was with. Remember?”

“Yeah.” Bee folded one arm and propped her fist under her chin. “That’s the most suspicious activity we’ve seen so far.”

“What do you think we should do?”

Bee was silent for a while, and the distant rush of water on the beach behind the Oceanside filled the gap. The salty sea air, the light filtering from between the curtains in the living room, and the scent of whatever Shawn had made for dinner this evening did nothing to comfort me.

Sam needed our help.

“Bee.”

"Stakeout," she said.

"This is hardly the time to go out for dinner."

"No, Rubes. A stakeout. Like a police stakeout. We're going to follow Millie and catch her with this stranger, and then we're going to find out exactly who he is and what he's doing in Carmel Springs."

It was the best plan we had.

Twelve

Millie's house was located on the corner of Lobster Way and Maple Street. The two concepts blurred in my mind, bringing me a strange need for a lobster roll drizzled in syrup. Or maybe that was the exhaustion.

We'd been posted outside of her house, across the street in a bush, for the past two hours. We were barely protected from the cold in our black coats—mine was woolen, and Bee's was leather and pretty cool, I had to admit—and my patience had worn thin.

"I'm cold," I whispered. "Are we even sure Millie is home?"

"The lights are on in the upstairs window," Bee said, without a hint of a tremor in her voice. Clearly, leather had better insulation qualities than wool. "She's home. And

73

that car parked out front isn't hers." She nodded toward the silver-gray Honda in the short driveway.

Bee's face was mostly in darkness, but the nearby lamp-post lit the side of it when she shifted and peeked out from behind the bush.

I sat with my legs crossed, picking grass from the ground, rolling it up and flicking it away. I stifled a yawn. "I don't want to be a brat, but this is super boring."

Bee sighed.

"And cold."

"Ruby, if we had a car other than the food truck, I would've suggested we perform the stakeout in that. But the food truck doesn't exactly scream 'undercover.'"

"Would it be wise to scream 'undercover' during a stakeout?"

"Hilarious."

Bee had a point. Whining wouldn't get us any closer to freeing Samantha. But it was still something to see—Bee so focused, her gaze fixed on the house across the street. You'd swear she'd done something like this before.

"How are you so calm?" I asked. "You seem completely relaxed about the whole 'stakeout' thing."

Bee opened her tote bag and removed a bottle of water and a Tupperware. Inside sat a collection of meringue topped cupcakes. "Here. Keep your energy up."

"Bee?"

"Yeah."

"Why are you so calm? Have you, um, have you done this before?" I asked.

Bee's fingers fumbled on the lid of her water bottle. "Yes," she said. "I don't make a point of talking to people about my past, but now that you ask, yes, I have done this before. I used to be a police officer."

My jaw dropped. I struggled to find words.

"You're shocked," Bee said, sounding bemused. "I guess that means I've done a good job of keeping my past private."

"I had absolutely no idea. I didn't know there was much overlap between baking and investigating."

"Neither did I," Bee said. "I got tired of working the beat. I lost a friend. A partner. And after that, I was done. Besides, I've always wanted to be a baker."

"Why didn't you follow your dream sooner?" I asked, hoping it didn't come across as judgmental. After all, I hadn't followed my dream from the start either. I'd let my love for Daniel command which career path I'd chosen.

"Because I wanted to fill my father's shoes. He was a decorated police officer and a fantastic man. To everyone else except for me. I wanted to impress him. But, the man's long gone, and I finally had the courage to do what I wanted to do," Bee said. "I'm only sad I didn't give myself a chance sooner. I should've told him to his face that I wasn't going to be what he wanted."

"Live and learn."

"True." We fell into an easy silence, and I tucked into one of the lemon meringue cupcakes, relishing the sweetness, the tang of lemon, and everything that went with it. It was absolutely divine and helped soothe away some of the aches and groans, even if that was just a mental thing.

Bee finished off her cupcake, drank some water, then lifted a pair of pocket binoculars out of her tote and pressed them to her face. "There's movement in there. She's definitely not alone."

"Who do you think the guy is?" We'd had this conversation again and again and come up with no real answers. It wasn't as if we could internet search "strange guy friends with Millie."

"We're going to find out, Rubes, don't worry." Bee lowered her binoculars. "I'm only sorry we couldn't have caught him before he did what he did to Detective Jones."

"Poor Jones."

"Hmm. Debatable. Not that he deserved to die, but he was such an abhorrent—"

"Shush! Look out."

The front door of Millie's house had opened, and two figures appeared. One was Millie, her gray hair loose around her shoulders, a fluffy robe tied tight around her waist. She had dark rings under her eyes and seemed downtrodden, her shoulders drooping.

The second figure was the stranger. The Al Capone if he'd gone on a diet and grown a few inches taller. He said something to Millie, towering over her, lifting a finger and waggling it. After, he strode down her front path and onto the sidewalk.

Millie shut her door, cutting out some of the light.

The stranger walked toward the corner, in the direction of the beach.

"Quick," Bee said. "Follow him."

We stuffed our things into Bee's tote then rose and raced down the street. We cut into another and found the suspect halfway across it, his hands tucked into his pockets, whistling under his breath.

What now? Where is he going?

Thirteen

The Mafioso led us down long streets and around corners. He paused under a lamppost to light up a cigarette then set to walking again, scuffing the soles of his shoes on the gritty cement and humming a tune.

"Where is he going?" I whispered.

We were further back, but it was better to be safe than to be discovered by a potential murderer.

Bee didn't give me an answer. Her hazel eyes glinted as we passed by the vignettes of light cast by lampposts. The chill was stirred up by the wind, and leaves skittered across lawns. We entered the street that led past the pier and the guesthouse, and I gasped.

"He's going to the Oceanside," I hissed.

The suspect froze mid-stride. He turned around and stared at us.

"Oh, I think he heard me," I said.

"There's no 'think' about it. He definitely heard you," Bee groaned.

The man removed the cigarette from between his lips and tossed it onto the sidewalk. He stamped it out with the underside of his Italian loafer. Of course, I didn't know if it was actually an Italian loafer, but it fit his personality. Or the assumptions we'd made about him.

"There a reason you're following me?" he asked, in a thick New York accent.

Oof, definitely part of the mob.

"Hi," I said.

"Hello," Bee echoed.

"We're just heading back to the Oceanside." I folded my arms. "And we noticed you were going that way too."

"You're a terrible liar," the guy said. "You should, uh, work on that if you wanna get ahead. You know. With whatever it is you're doing. Now, you'd better tell me why you're following me before I call the cops."

"You, call the cops on us?" Bee was suspicious. "We're not the ones stalking around town looking menacing."

"Menacing?" The guy laughed. "Last I heard, it ain't a crime to look any type of way."

"There was a murder at the guesthouse," I said. "You wouldn't happen to know anything about that, would you?"

The guy's laughter cut out. "Who are you?" he asked. "You cops?"

"No."

"Yes." Bee cleared her throat. "I mean, no. But that doesn't matter. We know you're up to something. We saw you with Millie, and she didn't look too happy about having you around."

"Of course she's not happy about having me around." He drew closer, swaggering, his shoulders and arms swaying. "I'm her ex-husband."

If my jaw could have dropped lower, it would have punctured the earth's crust and mantle and fallen right into the nickel core. "You're what?"

"Her ex-husband." He stuck out a tan hand. "Tony Malone," he said, saying the "Malone" like "Maloney." "Pleasure to make your acquaintance."

Bee shook his hand. I did too and found that his grip was strong. Maybe a little too strong. "What are you doing in Carmel Springs?" I asked. "I don't mean to be rude, but we didn't even know Millie had been married."

"Of course you didn't. Why would she tell anyone about her failures?" His lips parted in a sharkish grin. "I was coming down to this guesthouse to see if I could get a room for the night. Millie doesn't want me sleeping on her sofa, and I'm tired of sleeping in my car."

His car. The Honda. Why hadn't he driven here if he'd wanted to book a room? Suspicion bubbled inside me.

"Sam's not at the guesthouse. And you can't make a booking in the middle of the night," Bee said.

"All right then. I guess I can wait until tomorrow. You two have a lovely evening," he said and winked at us. He strolled past, whistling and taking his pack of cigarettes out of his pocket.

Bee and I stood quietly until he'd turned the corner.

"Good heavens," I whispered. "What was that about?"

"The lying?" Bee asked. "I don't know, but I don't buy that this Tony guy wanted to stay over at the guesthouse. Or that he's Millie's ex-husband."

"We could always ask her."

"How? Short of ambushing her while she's at work or out to eat, how will we ask her? She's been avoiding us like we're the flu."

I didn't have an answer. Instead, I looped my arm through Bee's, and we walked back to the Oceanside together. We stopped on the porch, and Bee brought her keys from the tote bag. "You know what I've been thinking?" she asked.

"Do tell."

"We haven't checked out any of the alibis for the people staying at the guesthouse."

My brow wrinkled. "What, you think that it was someone who lives here?"

"Obviously the cops thought so or they wouldn't have arrested Sam. What if the evidence has been staring us right in the face all this time, and we didn't even realize it?" Bee opened the front door, and we slipped into the warmth of the guesthouse.

I removed my woolen coat, unbuttoning it with ice-cold fingers. "What about Tony?"

"We don't have anything on him," Bee said, quietly. "He's still a suspect, of course, and so is Millie, but we need to focus on the people who were here on the night of the party. Jones was killed here. His body was placed in the living room on your gifts. It's got to be someone who had access to the guesthouse."

Food for thought, yeah, but it also pointed back to Sam as the one who'd done it.

Trouble's kitty meow drifted from the staircase that led to the second floor, and I switched on the hall light and smiled at the calico puff of fluff. "Hello, sweetheart. Do you want to sleep in my bedroom tonight?" The poor dear. And poor Sam, having to sleep in a jail cell, fearing for her future.

I could relate. Jones had dumped me in a jail cell over Halloween weekend because he'd decided my citizen's arrest was code for interfering in his murder investigation.

"Come on," I said, "let's get some rest."

"Fine," Bee replied. "But I suggest we hold a meeting with the guests over breakfast and establish some alibis. If they care at all about Sam and the guesthouse, they'll want to help us figure out who did this."

"Deal." I picked up Trouble and made my way to the second floor and into my room. I was too exhausted to take a shower before bed. I flopped down and fell asleep, drifting into dreams of strange tan men who talked like Don Corleone from *The Godfather*.

Fourteen

"Good morning, everyone," Bee said, standing next to the fireplace, her hands behind her back. She wore a smart blouse tucked into a pair of waist-high slacks and had paired her reading glasses with the outfit for effect. "How's the food?"

The Carlingtons smiled at her from their usual window seat. "Delicious as always," Mrs. Carlington said.

"Delightful," Kayla called out, from her spot in one of the armchairs. She had a habit of grabbing something she could eat with her hands rather than a knife and fork. She held a croissant over her plate and swept it through a puddle of jam. "Shawn's outdone himself again."

The chef, Shawn, stood next to the kitchen doors, leaning against the wall, his dark hair falling across his eyes.

We'd asked him to come into the room and hang

around. It was important. It was to help free Sam from prison, and since Sam was the one who'd given Shawn a second chance at turning his life around, he'd do whatever he could to help. And that was another reason I couldn't believe he'd have killed Jones either.

Why would Shawn have jeopardized his future?

"We need to talk to you all," I said, joining Bee, my heart skipping about twenty beats a minute. This was it. What if they got super angry with us for this? I didn't like upsetting people, but we had to do whatever it took to help Sam.

"About what, dear?" Mrs. Carlington asked, brushing off her neat flowery dress. She wore thick stockings with it, and a coat hung over the back of her chair. "I hope it won't take too long. We were hoping to get out there and go exploring today. The Lobster Shack has another special this week."

"As you may know," I said, "Sam has been arrested for the murder of Detective Jones."

Mr. Carlington dropped his fork, and it clattered onto his plate. "She what?"

"She was arrested yesterday evening just before dinner."

"I wondered where she'd gone," Mrs. Carlington said, faintly. "Poor woman. But did she really ... she doesn't seem like the type to..."

"We don't think she did it," Bee said.

"But then who did?" Kayla asked, leaning in and spilling croissant flakes across her lap.

"We don't know, but we have to start asking questions, because the police certainly aren't going to," I said. "We need to know what you saw. As guests at my party, you likely came into contact with the murderer. So, we'd like to ask you a few questions."

Kayla checked her watch. "I'm not sure I have time for this. I have to go train for my competition. My, uh, gym instructor will be expecting me."

"This won't take long," Bee said.

"Please, help us out. You guys are our only leads at this point."

"Meaning we're suspects?" Kayla's dark eyebrows rose.

"No, just that you might inadvertently be witnesses," I said.

"And suspects," Bee put in.

I palmed my face. She was incorrigible. It was easier to get information with honey rather than the stick, but Bee wanted the same result I did.

"We'll help in whatever way we can," Mr. Carlington declared. "What do you need to know?"

"We need to know where you were before the party and if you heard anything during it," I said.

"Oh, that's easy," Mrs. Carlington said, brushing

off her dress. "Before the party, we were at the Lobster Shack. We'd been dying to try out their new seafood chowder, and it didn't disappoint. And during... well, there was some noise after the lights went out, but I didn't realize what it was until we saw the body."

"Yes, that's right." Mr. Carlington clicked his fingers. "There was a sort of banging noise. I thought someone had fallen over, but it was quiet after that. So I figured everyone was OK."

"You couldn't see anything moving in the dark?" I asked.

All three of the guests and Shawn shook their heads.

"Well, I was on the beach before the party," Kayla said. "I go for a walk at that time every single evening. Good for stretching the muscles after a workout. I didn't hear any banging or thumping during the 'lights out' part of the party."

"I was here all day, setting up for the party. I heard strange noises upstairs a few times, but I didn't think it was a big deal. Figured it was just some guests getting ready for the party," Shawn said, shrugging.

"Is there anything else you've noticed around here?" Bee asked. "Anything strange or suspicious?"

The guests exchanged glances.

"Well, um, there is one thing," Mrs. Carlington said.

"It's silly, and I don't think it has anything to do with the murder, but my perfume has gone missing."

"Your perfume?" I asked.

"Yes. It was an anniversary gift from my dear husband." She reached across the table and squeezed his hand. "It smells of roses, and it was my favorite scent. It went missing a few days before the murder. I can't understand where it's gone since I put it right there on my bedside table."

Shawn grunted. "I've noticed the same thing. Kitchen stuff missing."

"Yeah," Kayla said, shifting in her seat and spilling more crumbs everywhere. "Totally. Um, my journal went missing. I use it to track my weight. But I didn't think it was anything serious, you know? It's just a calorie journal."

Now, that was strange. A thief and a murderer?

"Has anything else gone missing?" I asked.

"You mean, apart from my letter opener?" Bee countered.

The Carlingtons grew pale. Kayla sighed.

"Nothing for me," Shawn said. "But I keep my door locked at all times. I don't let nobody come near my stuff."

That didn't give us much information, other than the fact that Shawn didn't have a real alibi. Neither did Kayla, for that matter. Could either of them have done it? But what would the motivation have been?

"Thanks for your time, everyone," I said. "We'll try to get to the bottom of this one. The sooner, the better, right?"

"Right," the Carlingtons said, in unison.

And that was it. We had a few leads, but what if they didn't go anywhere? Our only option was to follow them and to talk to Millie about what had happened with her ex-husband. As far as I was concerned, the thieving of personal goods couldn't possibly be connected to the murder, could it?

Fifteen

I served another customer on the food truck, trying to put up a smile, but it was difficult, especially since Sam was behind bars. How were we supposed to concentrate when one of our closest friends was locked up unlawfully?

And none of the evidence pointed toward anyone else, either.

Shawn had had a fight with Detective Jones, but his DNA wasn't on anything—a relief, if I was honest, because we liked Shawn. And he'd been so good at recovering from his past transgressions.

Millie and her ex-husband were definitely up to something. Why on earth had he headed toward the guesthouse after talking to her? That didn't make any sense. And I didn't buy his story that he'd wanted to stay at the guest-house or check in so late at night.

"Rubes?" Bee poked me on the arm. "Are you all right?"

The customers had gone, and the sun was high in the noon sky. The cry of a gull punctuated the quiet after Bee's question.

"I've been better," I said, softly. "I just want us to figure this out. Where do you think we should look next?"

"I don't know," Bee replied and rubbed her temples. "It's strange to me that things have been going missing in the guesthouse. And that the body was dumped there like the killer wanted it to be found."

"Or maybe, they couldn't move it far enough away." I paused. "This means that Detective Jones was at the guest-house. Why do you think that is?"

"I have honestly got no idea. And that's what makes this even more frustrating." Bee stripped off her apron. "You know, I think we should—ooh!"

"You think we should ooh? That doesn't sound conducive to a successful investigation."

"No, I just got a text." Bee extracted her phone from the pocket of her high-waisted pants. "Oh, it's from Millie."

"What does it say?"

Bee tapped her screen. "She's asking to meet us at the

Lobster Shack tonight at six. She says she wants to explain what's been going on. She heard that we met Tony."

"We have to go," I said, immediately. "Maybe she needs help. Maybe Tony is manipulating her."

"As we initially suspected, yeah." Bee dragged her teeth over her bottom lip. "Let's do it. I'll text her back."

"Good. Do you think we should close up early?" I checked my filigree watch—it was already past four. "We might need time to prepare our questions and maybe snoop around the guesthouse a little. Especially if someone's been breaking in."

"Good idea." Bee sent off the text to Millie to confirm.

Quick as we could, we closed up the truck and headed back to the Oceanside, the sun glancing across the road and lighting our path, occasionally obscured by a cloud. Again, there was a storm on the away, hovering over the ocean, bruising the sky to black. How much longer until it broke?

I steered the food truck into our favorite parking spot and got out. The Carlingtons' car wasn't here, and neither was Kayla's. Maybe she'd finally gone to her competition. Though, how she expected to win after drowning herself in cookies and cakes all week was beyond me.

"It's quiet," Bee said.

"Don't say 'too quiet,' please. I've had enough drama to last me a lifetime."

Bee and I hurried up to the front door of the guest-house, and I drew the keys out of my handbag. But the door was already ajar, and the lights in the hall weren't on.

"Uh, what's this about?" I poked the door, and it creaked open.

"Creepy." Bee entered and clicked on the hall lights. "Shawn? Are you here?"

"Shawn?" I joined her.

That was odd. Shawn usually started preparing dinner by four, and there were no sumptuous smells drifting through the guesthouse. The hair on the back of my neck stood on end.

I walked into the living room.

Shawn lay on the floor on his side, his eyes closed, one arm trapped under his body and the other splayed out, fingers grasping as if he'd been reaching for something.

It took all my energy not to let out the gut-wrenching scream that gathered in my throat.

Bee rushed past me and bent next to the young man, whose hair had fallen across his eyes. "Shawn!" She pressed two fingers to his throat. "It's fine. He's alive. He's got a pulse. Shawn? Shawn!" She rolled him onto his back.

Shawn groaned. His eyelids fluttered and opened.

Relief flooded through my limbs and turned them into jelly. I stumbled and lowered myself to my knees next to him. "Oh my gosh. What happened?"

He tried to sit up, pushing himself up onto his forearms.

"Whoa, easy there," Bee said. "Don't move. We don't know what happened to you yet. You might hurt yourself more."

"Ow," Shawn said, settling back again and pressing his hand to his forehead. "That hurts."

"What happened?" I asked, breathless.

"I don't know. I don't remember. No, wait. I was in the kitchen, and I heard a noise out here, like someone, shuffling around or breaking something. I came out to check what it was, but there was nothing. I was just about to—ouch, sheesh that hurts." He squinted.

"You were about to…?" Bee prompted.

"I was about to go back into the kitchen when … I saw a flicker of something, and I smelled…"

I hung on the edge of his every word. "Yes? You smelled what?"

"Go on, Shawn. Tell us what happened." Bee's voice was much calmer than mine.

"I smelled roses. And there was movement behind me. I tried to turn, but then something whacked down on the back of my head. And that's all I remember." He winced again, sliding his hand over the back of his head. "I've got a bump. It's huge. Ow."

"I'm calling the police," I said.

"And an ambulance."

"No, I don't need an ambulance," Shaw replied. "I'm fine. I can stand." He tried moving but slumped back again, closing one eye. "Woo, when did the room start spinning?"

"Stay still," Bee said. "Rubes, you watch him while I call the cops."

"On it." I shifted closer to Shawn. I wasn't sure what the protocol was with concussions—which he likely had if he'd been struck over the head. But I'd read somewhere that falling asleep was against the rules. "How are you feeling?"

"Drunk," Shawn said. "And I haven't touched alcohol in a year."

"Oof. OK, don't worry, help is on the way, Shawn. We'll find out who did this to you."

A silence fell between us. Thankfully, Shawn's eyes didn't droop closed. "Do you think it was the murderer?" he asked.

How could I answer that? Either way, I had no idea. But Shawn had mentioned roses. He'd *smelled* roses. Hadn't Mrs. Carlington told us just this morning that her rose perfume was missing? Clearly, the thief, whoever they were, didn't want to be caught.

Something twigged in the back of my mind, but I couldn't quite place my finger on it.

"All right," Bee said, re-entering the living room. "They're on their way. Don't worry, Shawn. You're going to be all right."

"I bet whoever did this framed Sam too," Shawn said, his eyes wilder than usual. "You've got to find them. Please. For Sam."

Sixteen

THE LOBSTER SHACK WAS AS FRIENDLY AS I remembered it, with wooden tables, buoys hanging off the walls, and the scent of seafood on the air. Music tinkled from the speakers, and almost all of the tables were full.

A greeter emerged from behind a wooden podium and smiled at us. "Good evening, ladies. How may I help you? Table for two?"

"We're meeting someone, actually."

"Oh, Millie? She mentioned that two women would come by asking for her. She's out on the deck by the fireplace. Follow me." The greeter snagged two menus from the side of the podium and walked us through the restaurant.

Familiar faces were everywhere, and a few of the diners waved a greeting. It was difficult to return it with a smile after what had happened today. Poor Shawn was in the hospital with a serious concussion. Detective Martin had followed the ambulance, so it was clear that he thought something was up.

Did that mean that he'd free Sam? I couldn't possibly rely on that being true. We had to solve this on our own.

Gosh, I need to stop with the fatalism. It's not healthy for me. Neither were cupcakes, but I ate as many of those as I could get my hands on.

We exited onto the deck—a gorgeous wooden overlook that viewed the ocean and held little fairy lights along its balustrade. A central fire pit contained roaring flames, and the tables all around it were full. At one of them sat Millie, looking thin and wan in comparison to her usual jolly self. A folder rested next to her on the table, the top occasionally flapping in the wind.

"Here you go," the greeter said. "Your server will be with you shortly."

"Thank you so much," I replied.

We sat down across from Millie.

Her sharp blue-eyed gaze glimmered less than usual. "Hello, ladies," she said.

"Millie. It's been too long." I patted her on the back of the hand.

She flinched.

"What's wrong?" Bee asked. "Why have you been avoiding us? And what's up with that weird Tony guy?"

"You certainly know how to get to the point, Beatrice."

"No one would accuse her of beating around the bush," I said, trying for a weak laugh. It fell flat.

Millie leaned in, and we followed her example. "I asked you here today because I feel I owe you an explanation. I'm usually at the truck every day, and I would consider you both my friends. I think you're wonderful people, and ... well, it's just wrong of me."

"What is?"

"Lying to you."

"How did you lie to us?" I asked.

Millie withdrew a Kleenex and blew her nose into it—a foghorn blast. She dabbed underneath her eyes afterward. "I should have told you about my past, but now it's too late. Tony's going to tell everyone anyway."

"I don't understand."

"Me neither," Bee put in.

"Tony, my ex-husband, was once a part of the mob. But he was kicked out a long time ago. I divorced him back then, but it was already too late. He's spent years hunting me down so that he can blackmail me about my past. He wants money. Money I don't have."

Money. Would he steal? But no, I couldn't picture

Tony spritzing himself with Mrs. Carlington's rose-scented perfume.

"Why would you avoid us because of that?" I asked. "You know we don't care about your past. Everyone has their issues and secrets. As long as you didn't do anything illegal…"

"No, I didn't," she said, quickly. "But he knows that my reputation won't be able to stand a knock like this. I'm the editor of the paper, for heaven's sake." She tapped on the folder next to her. "And I'm too scared to go into work in case he follows me there and starts asking questions or saying things."

"Millie, it's simply ridiculous that you think people will care what he has to say," Bee said, brusquely. "He's an ex-con, and you're the editor of the paper. Everyone loves you. Heavens, we thought you were avoiding us because he had something to do with Jones's murder."

Millie gasped. "No. Good lord, if he'd killed Jones I would have reported him to the police immediately and gotten rid of him. Not like that. You know what I mean."

"Of course."

"I suppose you think I was involved somehow because of the article I wrote?" Millie asked. "The op-ed? That was because Jones had been stalking me for days, insisting that I tell him all I knew about you, Bee."

"About me?" Bee spluttered. "Why on earth would he be interested in me?"

"I have no idea, but he was practically obsessed. Like a dog with a—oh no!" The folder on the table had flapped open, and one of the pages escaped. It whipped up into the air. "That's our headline piece!"

"I've got it!" I jumped up and snatched after the paper. My fingers closed around its edge just inches before it was lost to the fire in the central grate. "There." I sat and smoothed out the crumples from my hasty grab. The title stood out.

Bodybuilding Competition Marred by Stealing Scandal

My insides did a flip.

"—you see, I wouldn't hurt a fly," Millie continued, "and I simply don't have time for my ex-husband either. But I don't know what to do about him."

"Let him say what he has to say, Millie. In fact, you could do one better," Bee replied. "You could write a tell-all expose about your past before he can say anything. Publish it in tomorrow's paper. Disarm him."

"You think that would work?"

"You have nothing to hide. You could frame it like

you've been manipulated by him," Bee said, conversationally. "Which you have."

"What's this?" I asked, lifting the page I'd caught. "About the bodybuilding competition?"

"Oh, that's our headline piece for tomorrow. Huge scandal. The competition was ruined because all the prizes were stolen from the venue after the competition ended. Before they could do the prize-giving ceremony."

"It's already happened?" I asked, frowning.

"Yes, over two weeks ago. Right after Halloween."

My mind clicked, almost audibly. "Oh, my heavens. Oh my gosh."

"What is it?" Bee asked.

"Rose perfume," I said. "Stealing. Bodybuilding competition theft. Kayla. It was Kayla. She hit Shawn. And she killed Jones."

"What? How can you possibly be sure?" Bee asked.

"She has no alibi, she lied about when the competition was taking place, and things have been going missing around the Oceanside."

Bee let out a squeak. "I'm stupid!"

"No, you're not," I replied. "But why do you say that?"

"Because she was wearing gloves on the night of the party. I still remember asking her whether she really needed to wear them indoors because she looked a bit like Michael

Jackson." Bee paused, wriggling her fingertips as Millie looked on. "No fingerprints on the murder weapon except for Sam's. And Sam was the one who equipped the room with the letter opener. Of course, her prints would have been on the weapon."

"We have to go," I said. "Now. Back to the guesthouse. If it really is her, we'll find that perfume that went missing in her bedroom. And the gloves, potentially blood-spattered."

Bee and I rose and sprinted from the restaurant, drawing a cry from Millie. It was too late to turn back now. We had to get to the guesthouse and stop Kayla from getting away.

Seventeen

IF I COULD'VE DONE A FANCY HANDBRAKE TURN into the parking spot in front of the guesthouse, I would have. The food truck simply wouldn't allow for it. And the time for fancy tricks and laughter was gone.

"Why do you think she knocked Shawn out today?" Bee asked.

"I don't know. Maybe because he was about to catch her doing something. Stealing something?" I leaped out onto the gravel in front of the guesthouse and ran for the front steps. I was up on the porch in seconds.

We crashed into the hall, but it was empty. The living room was too, the lights still on from earlier when we'd helped Shawn.

If it was Kayla, she sure had a lot to answer for.

"Second floor," I said, out of breath—I needed to start

a cardio regime if I planned on chasing after people like this. "Kayla's just down the hall on the left."

"She might be here," Bee whispered. "Maybe we should call Detective Martin."

"Her car's not outside. We'll call him when we have real evidence."

Together, we mounted the stairs and hurried past our bedrooms toward Kayla's. Shoot, we didn't have a key. What if it was locked?

I inhaled through my nostrils. A few weeks ago, I would never have burst into a bedroom after a murderer. Carmel Springs had changed me.

I tried Kayla's handle. The door opened.

"We're in luck," I whispered.

"That's weird. Why wouldn't she have locked it if she had something to hide?" Bee asked.

"Ever heard the phrase 'don't look a gift horse in the mouth?' It's a good one."

"Good heavens," Bee whispered, as we entered Kayla's room. "Solving crimes sure makes you spunky."

"I can't wait to clear Sam's name," I said. "Now, let's see what we've got here." I clicked on the bedroom light.

The bed was a total mess, the sheets pulled back and crumpled at the base of the mattress, and on it sat an open suitcase. Equally messy piles of clothing had been stuffed into the case, along with three gold medals and a trophy.

All around the room were things that didn't belong to Kayla. A crocodile-skin purse, the perfume that had gone missing, five silver forks, one knife, and two of the decorative statuettes that Sam kept in the living room.

"Wow," I said and walked over to the dressing table. On top of it was a collection of jewelry and wallets. "Wow. She's not just a petty thief, she's—"

The door slapped shut behind me.

I slued on the spot and came face-to-face with Kayla. Her lips were peeled back over white teeth that were too sharp to be normal. Had she gone and had them sharpened at the dentist or something? Seriously, she looked like a human shark. Her short dark hair stood upright, and she wore a pair of jeans, a black shirt, and a pair of leather gloves.

"You couldn't just wait until I'd skipped town," she hissed. "You had to come here, now."

Oh heavens, Kayla was a bodybuilder. She was probably stronger than Bee and I put together. And we hadn't called Detective Martin on the way over here, just in case we didn't find any solid evidence that it was Kayla who'd committed the crime.

"Now, Kayla," I said, putting up my palms. "Let's not jump to any conclusions or do anything rash."

"I killed the detective, and you know it," Kayla said.

"Well, that effectively throws the whole not-jumping-to-conclusions thing out the window," Bee said. "She's not as stupid as she looks."

"Bee, now might not be the best time to taunt the murderess."

"Is there ever a good time?" Bee asked, wryly.

Kayla's eyes flicked back and forth in her skull, from one of us to the other. "Talk as much as you want. No one's going to hear you scream."

"OK, that doesn't even make any sense," I said, backing toward the table that held the fork and the knife. Perhaps we could arm ourselves and fight our way out? "If you're going to say something before you murder someone, you should really make sure it's … you know, profound."

"Don't tell me how to murder," Kayla growled, advancing on us.

"I wasn't, I swear," I said. "I was merely telling you what to say before you do the murdering. There's a difference."

"Slight difference," Bee corrected.

"Thank you. That's helping."

Bee shrugged. "If there was ever a time to split hairs, now's probably it." She winked at me, leaning back casually against the dresser and closing a hand around the knife. "Don't you think, Ruby?"

"Bee, say the word, and we'll split all the hairs you want."

"And what word might that be?" Bee asked.

"Oh, I don't know. 'Now' will probably suffice."

"What are you two blabbering about?" Kayla snapped. "Shut up. You're giving me a headache."

"Are you sure it's not all the murdering and stealing you've been doing?" Bee asked.

"Why did you kill Jones? At least tell us that before you do the deed." I leaned back against the counter, copying Bee's casual posture. My fingers touched cool metal, and I shifted one of the forks against my palm. A better weapon than nothing, at least.

"What does that matter?" Kayla asked, narrowing her eyes. "You're trying to buy time."

"Kayla, you can't possibly kill us both at once. One of us will escape," I said.

"Watch me." She lunged toward us, her arms outstretched.

"Now!" I yelled.

Together, Bee and I dove as well, bringing out our makeshift weapons. My fork hit Kayla in the shoulder and bounced off, clattering to the floor. Bee's knife grazed her arm, but didn't draw any blood—a butter knife wasn't that dangerous. Go figure.

"Idiots!" Kayla hissed.

The door crashed open behind her, and Detective Martin came in, his gun up and aimed at the back of Kayla's head. "Freeze," he yelled. "Back away from the women."

And just like that, it was over. We were safe. The detective had saved the day, and the bodybuilder wouldn't squash us into jelly.

Miracles did happen.

Eighteen

Thanksgiving Day...

"THIS TURKEY IS THE MOISTEST I'VE EVER HAD," Bee said, spearing a slice on the end of her fork. "Shawn, you've outdone yourself. I'm grateful for your cooking."

Shawn, the consummate goth, blushed and cut a piece of the turkey off for himself. "It's the gravy, that's all."

"Don't be ridiculous." Bee chewed enthusiastically, brandishing her fork. "You're just a natural talent at this."

Weeks had passed since the last murder in Carmel Springs, and since Kayla Thatcher had been taken away in the back of a police cruiser. It was such a great relief to have Sam back at the guesthouse that I offered up my silent gratitude for her presence at the table.

Kayla had been wanted in three states for her crimes. Petty theft, grand theft auto, aggravated assault, and attempted murder. Apparently, Detective Jones had walked in on her stealing from Bee's room, and she'd turned on him, knowing that if he arrested her, she'd be put away for longer than just a night. She was an ex-convict turned bodybuilder, using a fake name.

"You're right, Bee," Sam said, stroking Trouble's furry ears. She was seated at the head of the long table in the center of the dining room of the Oceanside. A fire cast warmth and light over all of us. The perfect Thanksgiving setting with just the four of us and Trouble. "Shawn is fantastic. I honestly don't know what I would have done without you."

"Now might be a good time to go around the table and say what we're thankful for." I lifted my glass of orange juice. "I'm thankful for the lessons I've learned in Carmel Springs, and for naughty little Trouble, who both keeps me company and awake at night."

"I'm thankful for all of you," Sam said. "Though we're so different from each other, I feel like I've made true friends, and I'm so grateful for that."

"I'm grateful for the opportunity to work and live here," Shawn said, lowering his head and peering at his plate instead of looking at us. "Nobody ever gave me a second chance until you guys came around."

"I am grateful for this amazing food and the amazing company. And—"

A knock rattled the front door of the guesthouse, and I jumped then laughed at myself. I was used to shocking happenings in Carmel Springs. A knock shouldn't have set me off.

"I'll check who it is." I rose and hurried through to open up.

Detective Martin stood on the doorstep. "Hi," he said. "Sorry to interrupt your Thanksgiving. I just wanted to wish you well, and I have something for Bee."

"For me?" Bee popped around the corner. She was too inquisitive for her own good. "What is it?"

Martin drew an envelope from his pocket. "It's a love letter."

"Goodness. I'm flattered," Bee said, "but I'm a little too old for you, kiddo. You'd have better luck with Ruby."

"No, he wouldn't," I choked. "No, no you wouldn't." I turned to Detective Martin.

He laughed. "It's not from me. It's from Detective Jones."

Bee lost her words. I did too.

"Wh—? Huh?"

"Read it for yourself," Detective Martin said, holding

out the envelope. "I couldn't give it to you 'til now because it was in evidence. He wrote it for you and came by to give it to you on the day he was murdered."

I grabbed the envelope before Bee could—this was definite fodder for me to tease her later on—and opened it up.

Dearest Beatrice,

I know this letter will come as a shock to you, but it's something that I must get off my chest. You're not a leaf peeper. You're a princess. I've been trying to hide my emotions from you for quite some time, but I think you must know we have a connection. I see it in the way you stare at me whenever I come by the food truck.

I'm writing to let you know that my wife is planning a trial separation. I don't care about her anymore. I am more than ready to start an affair with you.

If you're ready to pursue this with me and fulfill your every desire, call me. My personal number is attached below.

Ever yours,
Nate. (Detective Jones)

My eyes grew wider with every passing sentence, and I handed the note back to Bee. She read it too, blinking rapidly. "What on earth? This was why he was at the guesthouse?" Bee asked.

"Yeah," Detective Martin replied. "It's terrible what happened to him, and just before you two could—"

"Don't you start with me, young man." She waggled the letter at him. "This is a lie. It's all a lie." She scrambled the letter back into the envelope and marched away without another word.

I barely kept my laughter at bay. Of course there was nothing funny about Jones's passing, but just the fact that he'd thought Bee was interested in him was bizarre.

"I'd better get going," Detective Martin said. "You have a great Thanksgiving."

"And you."

The detective turned to go.

"Wait, um, Detective Martin?"

"Yeah?"

"Would you like to join us for Thanksgiving? We've got plenty of food," I said.

He hesitated, a small smile playing around the corners of his mouth. "Sure," he replied. "I usually spent it at Jones' place."

"I'm sorry for your loss, detective."

"Thank you."

And just like that, we'd added another friend to our circle in Carmel Springs. I couldn't fathom how strange it would be to leave this town behind once we did decide to go. But that was a thought for another time.

Christmas was up ahead, and I just knew that it would be a merry one. The first one in years, in fact, that I'd share with people who truly cared about me. Wasn't it just so strange, they happened to be people I'd met only a few months ago?

We sat down to our meal. We laughed. We teased Bee about her letter.

The night wore on and quiet warmth settled around the Oceanside.

Life didn't get any better than this.

Follow Bee and Ruby to their next adventure, MURDER UNDER THE MISTLETOE. *Available at all major retailers!*

Turn the page to read the first chapter!

Murder Under the Mistletoe

CHAPTER 1

IF THERE WAS ONE THING I WANTED TO AVOID this holiday season, it was murder.

Well, surely everyone wanted to avoid murder in general, but after the past few months Bee and I had had on the Bite-sized Bakery food truck, it was a valid wish.

Since we'd arrived in Carmel Springs, Maine, we'd investigated not one, not two, but a total of four murders! Some of the investigations had been out of necessity and others because we'd fallen into the trap of wanting to know more.

Curiosity killed the cat. So far, the satisfaction hadn't brought anything but the icy weather.

Bee hummed under her breath on the truck beside me, wearing a Santa Claus hat with a bell on the end. It was our last day on the truck for the year, but only because there was a Northeaster on the way, and the locals had warned us that staying out here was more than foolish. Potentially life-threatening.

"Can you believe Christmas is only a few weeks away?" Bee asked as she prepared us each a cup of scalding hot coffee. "The year has flown. Thanksgiving is over. We've gotten to know everyone in this town, and I just can't..."

"What?"

"Nothing. I just realized what I what I sounded like," Bee said, showing me her signature gap-toothed grin. "I'm not an emotional person. It seems like Carmel Springs has softened me up. There must be something in the water."

"Or the lobster."

"Or that," she said and rubbed her gloved hands together. "Good heavens, it's like the air is ice out here."

"Do you want to call it a day?"

"We haven't even had our first customer yet, Rubes," she replied. "Are you all right? Feeling ill?"

"I'm fine. Just not used to the cold." And I had a strange feeling in the pit of my stomach that something was bound to go wrong soon. We'd had lovely peace and quiet ever since Thanksgiving. There had been no murders, crimes or investigations.

As much as I loved investigating them—that came with the territory after having been an investigative journalist—I would definitely have preferred that no one in town was harmed.

"Are you sure you're OK?" Bee asked, narrowing one hazel eye at me.

"I've got the tingles," I said.

"Hmm. Care to elaborate?"

"The investigative tingles."

"Meaning what?"

"That I feel like something's on the horizon. Something big."

"Well," Bee said, "that's because there is something big on the horizon, Rubes." She paused for effect, spreading her hands. "Christmas! And our Christmas party. As for anything else, I think the lack of sun is getting to you."

She was right about that. The sky was a dull gray, and the ocean was dark, the beach empty. The hours had grown longer as we approached the thick of winter. Maybe my apprehension was more to do with that and having to leave the wonderful Oceanside Guesthouse that we'd called home for so long.

The folks here had finally accepted us, and now we were going to leave on our next great baking adventure.

"Good morning." Millie's warm greeting cut across my negative thoughts. She pottered into view, wearing a thick coat and a pair of matching woolen gloves. "You two are brave coming out here. I don't think you'll be getting many customers on a morning like this. Ice in the air, ice in the veins."

"Agree," I said. "I was just thinking we should call it a morning."

"Mind if I get one of your candy cane cupcakes and a cup of hot coffee before you do?" Millie asked, removing the newspaper from under her arm.

"Coming right up," Bee said and set to work getting Millie's order together.

"Is that the newest issue of the paper?" I asked.

Millie waved the local paper around then slapped it down on the food truck's side counter. "That's right. This one's great. My writers worked extra hard, and I appreciate that, given that it's Christmastime. It sure makes my job easier." As the editor of the newspaper, Millie had her ear to the ground at all times. She was a great friend and resource.

Listen to me. I can't stop thinking in investigative terms. Good heavens, it's Christmas. I need to relax.

"Anything interesting happening for Christmas?" I asked.

"Oh, well, let me see," Millie said, opening the newspaper and laying it flat. The scents of roasted coffee drifted through the air, mingling with the cold bite of salt off the ocean. "There's the local carolers group looking for new members."

"Hard pass," Bee said. "In this weather? They must have a death wish."

"Ooh, don't say that." I grimaced.

Bee rolled her eyes at me.

"Let's see, what else. Ah yes," Millie said, fumbling to turn pages with her gloved fingers. "Mayor Jacobsen was recently re-elected."

"He was?"

"Yes, in November. Hotly contested too. It was the first time in years he had a competitor for the post," Millie said, "and that made things interesting and fun too. He actually looked nervous about finding out the results. So, he's having somewhat of a celebration for it. Though I don't know if you could call the Christmas tree lighting a celebration."

"Oh, I heard about that," I said. "They're doing that tomorrow night."

"Yeah," Millie replied. "Everyone's going to be there. Though I think most of them are going to see if anything happens."

"What do you mean?" Bee handed over the candy cane cupcake and cup.

Millie took a sip of coffee and smacked her lips. "Well, everyone's heard that the Babcock's on the prowl."

"I'm sorry, the...?"

"The Babcock," Millie said, somewhat mysteriously, with a wriggle of her silver eyebrows.

"Is that some type of mythical creature native to Maine?" Bee asked.

"Oh, no, no. Everyone knows that if there was a mythical creature, it would be a lobster-eating sea monster, not a land-dwelling creature," Millie replied and took a bite of her cupcake. She chewed slowly, clearly enjoying the growing suspense.

"Who is the Babcock?" I asked.

"Or what?"

"It's a 'who,'" Millie replied. "A 'him' to be more specific. He's the local butcher, Clayton Babcock. Everyone calls him 'the Babcock' because he's such a force to be reckoned with. And he thought he was too when he went up against Jacobsen for the position of mayor. But he didn't win."

"What's any of this got to do with the lighting of the Christmas tree?" Bee's brow wrinkled.

"Apparently, the Babcock is furious that he didn't get elected. He believes that there was some fiddling with the votes," Millie continued, "which is patent nonsense, of course. Everyone knows that the votes are counted electronically. We had a new system installed last year, on Mayor Jacobsen's urging."

Millie took another bite of her cupcake and chewed.

"The Babcock," she said, "threatened to chop down the Christmas tree because of his displeasure. The man really believes that laws don't apply to him. I have it on good authority that a few police officers had to attend to a disturbance at the butcher's shop a few days ago because he was making so much noise about it."

"Do you think he'll do something like that?" Bee asked. "Chop down the tree?"

"No one knows," Millie said. "But if he does, you can bet your bottom dollar I'm going to be there to see it."

"Count us in." Bee clapped her hands together. "Ruby needs something to cheer her up."

"Oh no. Why? What's wrong?"

I shook my head. "Nothing. I've just got the strangest feeling that something's going to go wrong. Maybe I'm being paranoid."

"Or you're predicting the untimely demise of the Christmas tree tomorrow night," Millie said, her sharp blue eyes glimmering. "I'll see you then, ladies." She waved goodbye and carried her cupcake and coffee back to her car. She left behind the newspaper.

I picked it up. The black and white picture of the decorated Christmas tree was front and center, Mayor Jacobsen standing next to it, grinning from ear-to-ear, his belly straining against a smart black coat. "Come on, Bee. Let's close up and go have a cup of cocoa."

"I thought you'd never ask."

"I didn't ask," I said, quizzically.

"Oh, you know what I mean." Bee whistled as she helped close up the truck, infected by the Christmas spirit. I wished I could've felt the same.

Want to keep reading? Grab MURDER UNDER THE MISTLETOE from any major retailer. Thank you for your support.

Craving More Cozy Mystery?

If you had fun with Ruby and Bee, you'll want to meet Sunny and her Aunt Rita's cat, Bodger. You can read the first chapter of Sunny's story below!

The cat was out to get me.

It sat on the top step of my auntie's cottage, its black paws placed neatly beside each other, its yellow eyes focused on me. Every time I tried taking a step up the front path, it would hiss, fur standing on end.

Now, I hadn't exactly been expecting a welcome wagon when I'd arrived in Parfait, Florida, at the crack of dawn, but this was ridiculous. An angry cat, humidity that had no right to exist at 5:00 a.m., and the depressing realization that all my belongings fit into one wheeled suitcase —boy, was I living the life.

I cleared my throat, and the cat flicked its tail.

Why had Aunt Rita never told me she owned a cat? Though, in this case, it seemed more like the cat was the one who did the owning.

"Auntie," I warbled. "I'm here!"

She'd expected me two days ago, but paying my ex-husband's debts had taken longer than I'd hoped. There had been complications. People who I hadn't even known had had dealings with Damon had come out of the woodwork, looking for handouts. A lot of them were Russian. And intimidating. And had told me if I called the cops, I would regret it.

Try not to get depressed this early in the morning.

"Auntie Rita?" I called.

The cat hissed at me again.

"Oh relax," I said to it, hoping that my shouting hadn't woken the neighbors. Parfait was a small, coastal town, and the last thing I wanted was to make enemies on arrival. According to Aunt Rita, the locals adored her café and were pretty laid back, unless you got on their bad side.

I took a breath and fiddled with the extended handle of my suitcase. This was absurd. I couldn't let a cat get in my way. Aunt Rita had invited me to stay at her house while I got back on my feet after the messiest, scariest divorce in history.

And, yeah, I had been through the wringer, but I

wasn't about to let a feline with an attitude problem prevent me from having a good start to my "revival."

Granted, my revival had so far comprised three sweaty bus rides and being hit on by a toothless man who smelled of bourbon and peanut butter. Interesting combination, I'd give him that.

"Aunt Rita." I tried one last time.

The cat meowed, showing off disastrously sharp fangs.

"Look," I said, directing myself to the cat, "I like cats. Pretty much every animal is great in my books, barring chickens. Long story." I waved a hand. "The bottom line is, I'm expected, OK? Aunt Rita knows I'm coming, so you can chill out."

Another disdainful flick of the tail.

Grow a pair of ovaries, Sunny, for heaven's sake. What's the worst that could happen? It launches at your ankles?

I *did* have tender ankles.

"OK," I said, "I'm coming up."

The cat had understood that, it seemed, because it rose on all fours and yowled like a bat out of the nether. It hissed and spat, clawing as I walked up the cute path that led to Aunt Rita's single-story cottage.

"Shoo!" I waved a hand. "Shoo!"

The cat streaked toward me, and I braced for clawed impact. It disappeared underneath a bush rather than inflicting flesh wounds.

"Huh, would you look at that," I murmured. "All hiss and no claws." I trudged up the front steps, grinning at my silly idiom, and stopped on the cutesy, floral-print welcome mat.

I rapped my knuckles on the front door. "Aunt Rita?" It was early, but my aunt usually rose with the birds. She had when I'd lived with her, and I doubted that habit had changed over the last twenty years. Shoot, every Christmas I visited she'd wake me up with coffee at 4:30 a.m..

Twenty years. Gosh, was I really *that* old?

Thirty-eight and back at Auntie's house, looking for a place to stay, broke as the day I left.

I knocked. "It's me, Sunny." Still no answer.

The house was quiet as the grave.

Uh oh. OK, no need to panic.

My aunt always kept a spare key in plain sight in case she wasn't home when I came to visit. She'd changed her hiding spot from under the mat to the potted plant hanging from the eaves about a year ago. That was after I'd pointed out that everyone kept their spare key under the welcome mat.

I dug around in the soil in the potted plant and extracted the key. I dusted it off, my nerves building.

Why wasn't she answering the door? And why was her cat acting so weird? And when on earth had she gotten a cat?

I let myself into the cottage's entrance hall. It smelled faintly of lavender and chocolate chip cookies, as it always did. The evil cat streaked past me into the house, hissing for good measure, and I shut the door.

"Auntie?" I called out and flicked on the lights.

The place was immaculate—polished wood floors, styled in teal and cream, with framed pictures of me and Aunt Rita along the walls, showing my progression from geeky teenager to woman.

"Where is she?" I scooted my bag into place next to an end table. My gaze landed on an envelope propped against a vase of flowers. My name was scrawled across the front in my aunt's looping handwriting.

I lifted it, frowning. Why would she leave me a letter and not call me if she had a reason for not being here? Then again, I was a few days late.

I slit the envelope open with my aunt's silver letter opener and slipped out a single sheet of folded parchment paper.

My heart tha-thumped in my chest.

Dear Darling Sunny,

If you're reading this letter, I'm long gone. I regret to inform you that I've decided to go on a cruise with a few lady friends. To the Bahamas! Can you imagine it? Me in the Bahamas, sipping Bahamian drinks and dipping my toes in the water.

Now, you might think I'm crazy for leaving Florida, which is basically a prime vacation destination, but I need a break.

It's for this reason that I'm leaving you in charge of the Sunny Side Up Café until I get back.

I nearly dropped the letter in shock. "What?" I had no experience running a business whatsoever. I had gone to college to get a business degree, but my studies had been cut short when I'd married Damon. Besides, I couldn't cook a meal to save my life! Except for maybe spaghetti, and even that was touch and go.

I straightened the page and kept reading.

Don't worry, dear, you'll have plenty of help. Just try not to burn the place down while I'm gone.

I'll be unreachable for a few days until we've settled in, at which point you'll be able to contact me via the number on the back of this letter.

Have fun! Live a little!

Sincerely,

Aunt Rita

P.S. I've already had my neighbors feeding Bodger, but if you could take over from them once you arrive, that would be perfect. Also, Bodger hates everyone except for me, so make sure to lock your bedroom door at night. He has a tendency to leap at people's faces when they close their eyes.

Each word in the letter was worse than the last.

I was alone in my aunt's house with a homicidal cat and a café to run. Talk about out of my depth. And what had she meant about having plenty of help?

A knock rattled the front door, and I jumped and nearly dropped the letter.

Want to read more? You can grab **the first book, MURDER OVER EASY,** on every major retailer!